I0623065

ABOUT THIS BOOK

In this sequel to *The Winged & the Wicked* and *The Ward & the Wanderers*, the spring fae's family is in trouble again in another Teeny Weeny fairy tale.

Relentlessly trying to get back to her simple Havenwood Falls life, Teeny Weeny Tahini enjoys nothing more than her morning teas at the Broastful Brew with Mayor Barbie Stuart. But that seems to be where she always is whenever trouble comes into her life. This time it's a tantalizing Asian gentleman, a world-famous professional gamer who's wooed the local teens. But is tantalizing the right word? Mr. Wu has all of Teeny's senses on full alert.

When her friend Nina—the woman she hopes her nephew will propose to—suddenly disappears, Teeny is certain Mr. Wu has the answers. She never expects what she learns, though, and now it's up to her to save not only Havenwood Falls, but an entire dynasty of another place and another time. But first she must master her father's wand she'd recently found—and figure out her feelings for the Wu.

HAVENWOOD FALLS BOOKS

Forget You Not by Kristie Cook

Old Wounds by Susan Burdorf

Fate, Love & Loyalty by E.J. Fechenda

The Winged & the Wicked by T.V. Hahn & Kristie Cook

Alpha's Queen by Lila Felix

Ink & Fire by R.K. Ryals

Lose You Not by Kristie Cook

Tragic Ink by Heather Hildenbrand

Nowhere to Hide by Belinda Boring

Flames Among the Frost by Amy Hale

Rock Me Gently by Susan Burdorf

From the Embers by Amy Miles

Defying Gravity by Kallie Ross

Break Me Not by Kristie Cook

How the Dead Lie by Stacey Rourke

The Lurkers Within by Danielle Bannister

The Collector: Awakening by Kristie Cook, R.K. Ryals, Belinda Boring & Nadirah Foxx

Addicted to You by Belinda Boring

Affliction Mine by C.J. Pinard

The Ward & the Wanderers by T.V. Hahn

Toil & Trouble by Melissa Wright

Of Salt and Stars by Seven Jane

Redefined by Morgan Wylie

Betrayal Among the Frost by Amy Hale

Forever Loyal by E.J. Fechenda

Fate's Demand by Emily Cyr

The Wu & the Wand by T.V. Hahn

A Demon's Redemption by JD Nelson

Also try the YA line, Havenwood Falls High; the historical paranormal line, Legends of Havenwood Falls; the darker, sexier side of town, Havenwood Falls Sin & Silk; and the local supernatural college, Sun & Moon Academy.

Stay up to date at www.HavenwoodFalls.com

BOOKS BY T.V. HAHN

The Winged & the Wicked (with Kristie Cook)
The Ward & the Wanderers
The Wu & the Wand

THE WU AND THE WAND

T.V. HAHN

Copyright © 2019 T.V. Hahn, Ang'dora Productions, LLC

All rights reserved.

Published by

Ang'dora Productions, LLC

5621 Strand Blvd, Ste 210

Naples, FL 34110

Havenwood Falls and Ang'dora Productions and their associated logos are trademarks and/or registered trademarks of Ang'dora Productions, LLC.

Cover design by Regina Wamba at reginawamba.com

Except as permitted under the U.S. Copyright Act of 1976, no part of this publication may be reproduced, stored in a retrieval system, or transmitted in any form or by any means, electronic, mechanical, photocopying, recording, or otherwise, without written permission of the owner of this book.

Please do not participate in or encourage piracy of copyrighted materials in violation of the author's rights. Purchase only authorized editions.

This book is a work of fiction. Names, characters, and events are either products of the author's imagination or are used fictitiously, and any resemblance to actual persons, living or dead, is entirely coincidental.

To my friend Angela, whose enthusiasm for the story kept me writing, to my niece Kristie, whose belief in my storytelling encouraged me, and to my husband Paul, who Wu's me with his own kind of magic.

PROLOGUE

The bedroom chamber was still as night, though it was only slightly darkened by the oncoming twilight. Four people were in the chamber: the young boy (the poor soul who brought us all here in the first place, or so we thought), his mother, his father, and myself.

A straw of hay rustled across the rice paper floor. That was the only sound that could be heard for what seemed an eternity, until the stillness was interrupted with the eerie raspy rattle of death emitting from the frail body, of whom we stood by the bedside. His skin was waxen and yellow, and so chilled to touch that it numbed one's fingers.

The child had not moved for what felt like a century, but was most likely two or three days. Not a single movement could be detected underneath his sleeping eyelids. That at least might have given us an indication that he was still aware . . . maybe still with us.

Suddenly, the booming command came: "YOU MUST CURE HIM!"

Regardless of the strength of the command, it was easy to discern that it contained worry and grief, and even more—concern for the future of our world.

"Your Highness," I spoke slowly, trying very carefully to phrase the rest of my response so as not to anger but to do my job, "this is no illness I am familiar with." I paused.

"WHY ARE YOU HERE, THEN, IF YOU CANNOT CURE HIM? YOU SHALL BE EXECUTED AT SUNRISE FOR YOUR INSOLENCE AND DECEIT!"

"Your Highness, I am not speaking from either insolence or deceit. There is another force that is upon us. I don't believe this is an illness, but a curse. Someone or something does not want the young prince to survive." And then I bowed my entire body as low to the floor as I could possibly flatten myself.

It must have worked, because fortunately the ruler wavered. It was evident that the poor child had become afflicted too quickly and with no rhyme or reason for its onset. A curse may very well have been the cause.

"WHAT DO YOU NEED?"

"Your Highness, I need time"—the ruler lifted his staff, indicating he had heard enough, but I continued as quickly as I could—"which, of course, I am keenly aware that we do not have. But I have a method of overcoming that." I prayed under my breath. "My devotion and divination with Spirit Crane has put me in good standing with the spirit, and I believe She will assist me in finding out who placed the curse, and, to that end, how to break it!"

The rulers, having reigned so long and becoming so arrogant as such royalty tended to do, had lost their touch with the people. The child prince, however, was blessed with the knowledge and the gifts of his ancestors, and the people loved him. I loved him.

If he died, the people would revolt against not only the rulers, but the mysteries of mankind, and this realm would dissolve into shreds of nothingness.

But that was not my only challenge. I loved him, and I loved my people, but I loved this world too. I wanted—I *needed*—it to survive. There was something very dark, dangerous, and deadly out there, and I needed to use everything in my powers to find it and eradicate it.

CHAPTER 1

TEENY WEENY

It was another perfectly crisp October morning. I absolutely loved this time of year. It was invigorating. The harvest of all the delicious squashes—pumpkins, crooknecks, hubbards, and the like—had come in. There was such an array of colors upon us—the orange maples, the golden-leafed aspens, and of course all of the luxurious evergreens, from the bristlecone pines to the elegant spruces —all of them emitting a fragrance that I could feel.

Havenwood Falls, this small frontier-like town nestled in the cradle of a canyon and cloaked with the mystery of supernaturals and humans cautiously, carefully coexisting, was at its autumn peak, ready to burst with harvest and a few chills and thrills for the Halloweeners.

I grabbed my wool scarf, the latest one given to me by my nephew Mat and his girlfriend Nina, and headed out for my regular rendezvous with my best friend, Barbie a.k.a. Mayor Stuart.

Ah, Mat was not really my nephew, but a cousin. However, with hundreds of years between us, he had always known me as Aunt Siobhan.

My townhome, which housed my palm-reading salon, opened up to the south entrance of the square. I crossed over Main Street, and since we started our rendezvous fairly early in the morning, it was an easy crossing with no traffic. Town Square Park was accentuated with a fountain in its center. Some modern-day folks didn't believe the story that it was rimmed with real gold flakes that spilled from the floors of the gold-traders, some of whom founded this Havenwood Falls in the first place long ago during the gold rush. I was there, so I knew it was true.

As I approached the Broastful Brew, I could already see the mayor sitting at our familiar table.

The Broastful Brew was more of an artifact, kind of like me, than the best coffee shop in Havenwood Falls. Mabel, the owner and operator, landed in Havenwood Falls maybe twenty or thirty years ago. She was perfectly human, if there was such a thing, but that was what she was. I didn't know if she was one of those souls that were actually summoned to come, or if she just came here by happenstance. I suspected the latter. But you never knew.

The tinkle of the shopkeeper's bell rang a simple chime as I opened the door to the Brew. The flowery scent of Dragon Well green tea smacked me so hard in the face that my fingertips started to tingle, as did the tips of my toes. A distinguished Asian fellow lifted his head from the steaming cup of green tea, noting my entrance. He was very handsome with a neatly trimmed Fu Manchu and dark eyes that seemed nearly black. He appeared to be around my age, my glamour age anyway, but it was hard to tell, especially since I sensed in his eyes something much older, ancient even. I felt he may have been an old soul, reincarnated many times.

I nodded at him, hoping he would accept the greeting, and not think of me as too rude for my intense observance of him, then hurried to the back of the Broastful Brew to join the mayor.

"Good morning, Barbie! Boy, that Manchurian tea still has my fingers and toes tingling!"

"Good morning yourself! Are you sure it's that tea making you tingle?" Barbie winked at me and continued, "You were certainly examining that man up and down. He's really quite handsome, don't you think?"

I sat down, then leaned over the table as far as my four-foot-five frame would allow. Barbie obliged and leaned over her side of the table, meeting me more than halfway, her lemon chiffon bouffant bouncing on the top of my head.

"Who is that chap? Looks can be deceiving, you know, especially in Havenwood Falls," I said in a whisper.

"Don't I know it! Look at us! You have more power in your right pinky fingernail than I do from my heel to the top of my beehive. But anyway, that's Tim Wu, Dr. Wu. The Court invited him all the way from China. Don't you remember the discussion?"

"Well, sort of . . . He's some kind of a professional gamer, right? Well, that sounds pretty much like a professional gambler who already lost a couple of letters. I kind of tuned the whole thing out."

"He's more than just a professional gamer, though all the kids in town are excited about the Grand Master being here because of that. He's also a game developer, and his newest game *Rage of Realms* has an interesting premise—dark forces trying to destroy all magic. The Court felt we may be able to glean something from him."

Then the mayor abruptly straightened up in her chair and said, "That reminds me! Siobhan, you really have to consider being on the faculty of the Academy's College of Guardians. Adelaide is teaching one of the potions classes right now, and you know she's probably not the best choice for that subject. Not compared to you. We need you desperately!"

"I really don't think so, Barbie. I'm no teacher. Even after hundreds of years, I feel I am still a student myself, bumbling around this mysterious world."

My nephew Mat came to the table, carrying my usual chamomile tea. He'd been working morning shifts at the Broastful Brew pretty much since he arrived here two years ago.

"Good morning Mayor, Madame Tahini." He winked at me. *What's with all this winking this morning?*

Mat set down the teapot, steeper, and cup, and no sooner did he leave than the Asian gentleman approached the table.

"Good morning, ladies. I hope I'm not interrupting." He spoke in a smooth voice, but his accent seemed out of place, more British. Maybe he grew up in Hong Kong?

"Dr. Wu! A pleasure to see you this morning. Are your quarters comfortable?" the mayor greeted him, then turned to me. "Our guest is staying in one of the cabins at Whisper Falls Inn."

"And who is this charming little woman with you, Mayor?" Dr. Wu asked.

"I'm sorry. I've forgotten my manners! Dr. Timothy Wu, this is Teeny Weeny Tahini, I mean Madame Tahini, our resident palm reader and healer."

"Enchanted to meet you, Madame Tahini. I've dabbled a bit in healing divination myself. It would be a pleasure to share a spot of tea with you sometime, if you would care to join me."

Oh, dear. The tingling sensation started again, and this time it wasn't the tea, and wasn't just my fingers and toes—it extended to my earlobes, the back of my neck, even my nose!

"I would be delighted," I responded, not having any idea where that came from.

"How about four o'clock tomorrow afternoon? I'll meet you at the inn?"

"Oh, uh, four o'clock . . . tomorrow?" I stammered, trying to backtrack now and regain my composure.

"She'll be there!" the mayor piped in, giving me no room to renege.

"Brilliant! I will see you then." Dr. Wu nodded a goodbye and left.

The bell dangling from the front door tinkled again as the esteemed *doctor* left the shop.

Mat returned to the table and asked if we needed anything else. The mayor requested another cup of coffee, but I was still bouncing my tea steeper in my pot, trying to make heads or tails of what had just occurred.

"By the way, Aunt Siobhan, I'd like to show you the gift I got Nina for our second anniversary. I'll come by after my shift is over?"

Mat meant the second anniversary of their meeting and dating. It was a very slow romance in the making. Mostly because Nina, a very talented Italian tailor, was still quite gun shy because of the death of her lover many years ago.

"That'll be fine, Mat. I'll be home."

The mayor got up from the table and bade me farewell, again asking me to consider the Sun and Moon Academy's new College of Supernatural Guardians. I just shook my head. She was persistent, part of the great politician in her.

I finished my tea in solitude, swirling the brew in my cup and wondering what the tea leaves would be telling me about the town's new guest.

CHAPTER 2

TEENY WEENY

*A*fter my morning stroll through town, I returned home. I decided I'd better do a little homework regarding Dr. Timothy Wu, so I didn't sound like a complete dunderhead at tea tomorrow. Professional gamer? What was that?

I was intrigued about his healing divination comment, though I wasn't exactly sure how one "dabbled" in it. I decided I would start there in my research, since it sounded like something we may have had in common.

I went into the salon and perused my bookshelves. Wonderful leather-bound books filled every slot available, some with colorful ribbons marking important pages of note. Ribbons that the pixie sisters gifted to me regularly as a sign of their devotion.

I fetched the librarian's ladder stationed at the far end of the bookcases and glided it over toward the center. I was grateful for the ladder, as at least three of the shelves would be otherwise unattainable to me, though of course my friend Barbie could reach up and pull anything off even the tops of the cases.

On the second shelf from the top was a leather-and-silk-covered book with calligraphy along the spine reading, *Ancient Arts and Mystics*. A good place to start when delving into the arts of the Orient. I took the book and stepped down off the ladder, placing it on my salon table. The embroidered silk inlaid in the leather depicted a scene with cranes, bamboo, and a tiled-roof temple nestled in a thick forest.

I slid my finger down the table of contents and found the location for "Wizards of the Orient." My fingertip began to tingle once again. *A sign? Of what, I wonder?*

Opening up to the first page of the chapter, I began reading:

"The Wizards of the Orient date back well into the twelfth century BC. The earliest reports treated them as shamans, but as their skills in alchemy, herbal toxicology, and even martial arts developed, they became much more respected, and the royal houses often regarded the wizards, known as the Wu, as high officials, relying on their advice as well as their ability to divine spirits and heal the sick."

Wu. That's interesting, actually even kind of funny . . . Dr. Wu? Wu Who? Dr. Who? Wu.

Right when I was getting hold of my silly sidetrack and going back to my reading, the large metal knocker on my door alerted me to a visitor. Before I could even get to the foyer, Mat was coming through the entryway, bent nearly in half, since he was about six four. Upon each shoulder were two pixies, swinging their feet and taking turns hollering, "Giddy-up."

Once clear of the threshold, he straightened up and brushed the little imps off his shoulders. The pixie sisters simply rolled off him like lint balls, then abruptly began wrestling one another once they hit the floor.

Mat just shook his head and laughed. "Seems I attracted a few hitchhikers."

He bent over once again to give me a kiss on the cheek as I waved him into the living area at the end of the foyer.

We sat down before the fireplace, dormant now, as the weather had not become so chilled that it required a blazing hearth.

"Well, let me see it. Stop keeping your aunt in suspense!" I begged him to reveal the gift he had for Nina, hoping, just hoping, this was it.

He reached into his pocket, pulled out a small box, and handed it to me.

"I got it at Callie's Consignments. Nikita, Callie's cousin, is manning the store, and she just received a new shipment of artifacts from Callie herself. I couldn't resist this one."

I opened it slowly, because really I do like a *little* suspense. The tiny box revealed a golden pendant, the center of which displayed the yin-and-yang motif. Around the edge of the pendant was an array of Chinese characters, most likely an ancient wish or blessing. I turned the pendant over, and the back seemed similar to the front side, but the yin and yang had melded into a solid dark gray color. It too had script around the edge, but even though I didn't read Chinese—Mandarin, Cantonese, or otherwise—I could tell they were not the same characters as on its opposite side. As I touched it, my fingertips, rather than tingling, received tiny shocks, a little like pin pricks, but something more that I couldn't really distinguish. I wasn't really comfortable with this gift he had for Nina, but I didn't want to break his heart.

"Mat, it's really quite beautiful, and maybe something more . . . but don't you think it's time to give her a ring? You know, the type that goes on a certain finger, like a diamond ring?"

"I would love to, Aunt Siobhan, but I don't want to spook her. After that Valentine's Day debacle, I want to take it as slowly as she needs. I love her madly, but I want her to love me madly back."

"That sounds like yin and yang to me, then. In the meantime, let me give it a little blessing to protect it, her, and your love. I'll be right back."

I headed upstairs to get my father's wand—I mean, my wand. I didn't know what it was, but there was something about this amulet that made me uneasy. Maybe, if I got the chance, our illustrious guest, Dr. Wu, would be able to tell me what the script read.

I'd been keeping my special box in my bedroom ever since I discovered that it was originally made to hold the wand. I discovered so many things on that trip to the Isle of Gwynf'l and back last spring, but the box and the wand seemed to have opened up a whole new understanding of my life, my family, and maybe even my destiny.

I passed my hand over the box, tripping the keyless mother-of-pearl latch, and opened the box. My fingers still prickling, I fumbled a little with the wand, but as soon as I held it tightly in my hand, the tip began to glow and the prickly feeling disappeared.

I returned to the parlor only to find that the pixie sisters had moved their wrestling match to the rug in front of the fireplace. *Don't they ever get tired of this? Really, this has been going on for centuries now.*

I picked up the amulet once again, waved the glowing wand over it and under it, and chanted these words:

"Gods, goddesses, and spirits above

Grant this amulet with purest love

For whom its mystery is to be worn

Protect the soul that it adorns

Should anyone dare to steal its grace

This amulet shall remain in place

For all the fae that know—time will tell

Only one's true love can break this spell."

The tip of the wand grew brighter and brighter, and suddenly a flash came from it, enveloping the amulet, and then it extinguished as quickly.

Well, I hope that works.

"Thank you, Aunt Siobhan. I know that makes this gift especially worthy."

"Mat, may I take a picture of it with my phone? Maybe Dr. Wu can decipher some of this writing. I'd like to show it to him."

"Oh, of course. I forgot you are having tea with him tomorrow."

"Does everyone know my business here?"

"No, no. I just couldn't help overhearing the conversation. Broastful Brew is a small shop and isn't exactly bustling, if you know what I mean. By all means, take a picture."

I grabbed my cell phone from my skirt pocket. Of course, all my skirts have pockets for that very reason. I fumbled with the phone, since I particularly use it to call Barbie, and nothing else, but Mat gently took the phone from me, touched the camera icon, and snapped a photo of the pendant.

"Well, dear nephew, thank you!"

He also showed me where to find the photo he just snapped on my phone. That was smart thinking, because I wouldn't have had a clue.

The pendant placed back in the box, Mat popped the box back into his pocket, then asked, "Well, what about that position teaching at the College of Supernatural Guardians? Are you going to take it?"

Suddenly, the pixies stopped their wrestling and began their yammering.

"You have to be a teacher, Siobhan!" shouted Enya.

"Look at how much you've taught us," added Aeri.

"I want to be your pupil!" emphasized Tierri.

"Haha! I already have two pupils. That makes me a teacher, right? Get it?" Ushka broke out in a huge kind of gurgling laughing fit over her own joke. Needless to say, the remaining pixies joined in the laughter, rolling on the floor, only to be followed by, well, you know.

CHAPTER 3

WU

I knew the amulet was here. I could feel it all the way down to the marrow of these bones. But there was so much interference in this town. There was a lot of magic here, much of which I could not even identify.

Ah, these bones. Such a handsome young man, this Timothy Wu. I hoped he didn't mind that I was borrowing his body for a few weeks. If he was as great and as busy as these people said he was, then he probably needed the sabbatical I was giving him.

The mayor was quite a woman of stature, but it was the tiny woman, Madame Tahini, who concerned me some. She was an ancient. That I was sure of, yet she seemed to be an ingénue at the same time. She was definitely not from any area that I was familiar with, which was why I was pretty sure Tahini was not her true surname. I could not really pinpoint her talents, her knowledge, or whether she could be trouble. Nevertheless, I would stay on my guard, and try to get to know more about her.

I was to meet the little lady in just about an hour. I noticed she was extremely sensitive to smells. Her reaction to the green tea was more than noticeable. I suspected she had synesthesia, as did I. So I wanted her to relax and feel that she could trust me. Chamomile and lavender, I believed, would do the trick. I formulated a cologne of those fragrances.

~

As I headed over to the main building of Whisper Falls Inn from my cabin, I passed what Miss Petran called the conservatory. It looked inviting. Entering into the inn, I headed toward the front parlor, and there she was, such a demure little being. I should not have felt so threatened by her, yet I did. Perhaps, if it were not for this mission, I would have been sensing something else instead, or maybe that in itself was the threat.

"Madame Tahini! Such a pleasure once again."

She did not rise from her seat, but she lifted her hand. *Should I shake it or kiss it?* I took the lithe appendage into my own hand, covering it with my other and letting her feel that I was genuine with my words. *And really, I think I am.*

"As you, Dr. Wu. Tea?" she asked as she slowly withdrew her hand from my embrace.

I took a seat in the overstuffed chair across the coffee table centered in the parlor. "I suspect that you enjoy the Dragon Well green tea, so I took the liberty of having that prepared for us this afternoon. Is that satisfactory to you?" I said.

"It will be a treat, thank you. Maybe I will even get a chance to read your tea leaves before twilight."

"That would be a treat, I am sure." *Actually, it would not, especially if she does have prophetic abilities. I'd better make sure the leaves leave no clue.* "I also managed to smuggle in a flask of Tiger Pond water, so I've requested Michaela to steam the tea with it."

The lovely little lady bowed her head in appreciation. "I am honored to be treated like such royalty. Thank you, Dr. Wu." Her voice was like the song of a nightingale—pure and sweet. It suited her perfectly.

The owner of the inn, Michaela Petran, entered into the parlor at that very moment, with small cups of the steaming brew. There was a scent about the young woman that I couldn't exactly place. It was almost sanguine, but there were undertones of something else. It was possible she was among the creatures in this town that were interfering with my trying to position the exact whereabouts of that elusive amulet.

Michaela—or Kales, as I heard her friends refer to her—shakily placed the tray of tiny tea cups on the table in front of us. She seemed nervous or excited, but I guessed it was this Tim Wu personage I had taken on that had her and so many of the younger folk in town aflutter. Apparently he was a high-tech genius of some sort, and quite the rave around the world. Lucky for me, he came from the Wu clan, making it possible to climb into his skin.

"Miss Petran, by the heady bouquet, I can tell you have brewed the tea to perfection. Thank you for your kind attention."

The young woman was undoubtedly grateful for the compliment, explaining she was nervous about steaming the exotic tea, but after some research, a.k.a. googling, she felt more comfortable.

We engaged in the customary chitchat over tea. Madame Tahini told me a bit about the history of the town, but nothing too enlightening. I told her my family was from Hangzhou, which was actually true, though not in a contemporary sense.

Once we had finished imbibing in the luxuriousness of the tea, she reminded me that she wanted to read the leaves in my cup. I reached for the small vessel to hand to her, and pretended to accidentally knock it over, jostling the leaves around, altering their original arrangement at the bottom of the cup.

"Madame, I'm so sorry. I'm afraid that I've destroyed my own fortune, or at least the telling of it."

"No worries, Dr. Wu. Sometimes the happenstance is supposed to occur. Let me look." She picked up the porcelain demitasse and looked inside. "Hmm . . ." She paused. "And sometimes not. Oh, well, perhaps another time."

"Would you like to take an amble through the conservatory? It appears that there are some interesting plants there." Although our tea had concluded, I felt a tug to spend more time with her. I'm not sure if it was because I sensed she may know something about the amulet, or just because I was enjoying her company.

"Sounds wonderful. It's been a long time since I've stepped foot in it."

The two of us departed the parlor and walked through the dining room and the French doors that opened onto the conservatory. As we entered the sun-warmed glass building, there was an intense contrast to the cold, crisp mountain air. I found this exhilarating.

We walked around admiring the plant life that grew profusely in the domed structure, and I prodded Madame Tahini to tell me about her family. She told me she had a nephew who was really a cousin, who came to live with her a couple of years ago. In fact, he was the server at the Broastful Brew, and he had met a young woman here in Havenwood Falls who had captured his heart. In fact, she went on to tell me, he recently found an oriental pendant that he intended to give her in a day or two for their "sort of" anniversary.

"Oh! I almost forgot!" she said, and started hopping from one foot to the other excitedly while pulling a cell phone out of her skirt pocket. *How cute.* "I have a picture of it I wanted to show you. There are characters around the rim of it. I think they are Chinese, and I thought maybe you would be able to translate it."

Aha! I was right. That tug was telling me she knew something, but this was even better. *As long as I can see the etchings, I may not require the amulet itself.*

She pulled up the picture on her phone, fumbling a bit, as if she were new at this. I was about to assist her, but she managed it herself and held the phone up in front of me.

"Interesting . . ." I said as I pinched my thumb and index finger on the phone, then spread them to make the image larger. This knowledge I seemed to have gained from taking over Timothy Wu's body. His technological savvy had apparently melded into my mind. The photo on the screen showed the dark side of the amulet, the side of which I was already too keenly aware. "Is there an opposite side to the pendant, Madame Tahini?"

"Well, yes, there is, but I only took a shot of this side. Can you tell me what it says?"

Ugh, this is not good. I had to see the other side. I pretended to examine the photo in detail, turning the phone and enlarging each quarter of the circular pendant. "Madame, it is indeed Chinese, but it is a very ancient script. One I am not too familiar with. It seems to be about mythological creatures and spirits. Utter nonsense, of course, but I imagine so many eons ago, they seemed real enough."

I guess this meant I would be having my morning tea at the Broastful Brew tomorrow to have a chat with this nephew of hers.

"Dr. Wu, thank you so much for the tea and the stroll, but it's getting late. If you'll forgive me."

"Allow me to walk you home, Madame." *Maybe that Mat is at her place right now, and I won't have to wait until the morning.*

"Thank you very much, but it's only a half a block from here, and of course Havenwood Falls is quite safe." Then she hurried out of the conservatory, quickly taking a shortcut from the entry to the dining room heading directly to the corner of Beaumont and Eleventh.

CHAPTER 4

TEENY WEENY

It was kind of Dr. Wu to offer to walk me home, but after a couple of hours in his presence, all of my senses, including my sixth sense, were charged up. Walking the half a block from Whisper Falls Inn down Beaumont gave me a chance to let the frosty evening air clear up some of the sensory overload.

As I opened the wooden gate leading into my backyard, I saw Cyllene waiting for me on the windowsill. Her iridescent green wings, so much like a lunar moth's, glistened even in the fading light. I was glad that the little dryad was here, as I wasn't sure all the feelings I was having were going to wait until my morning brew with Barbie.

"Good evening, Silly Annie! So good to see you. Come in." I invited my dear old (like really old) friend into the house as I opened the back door to my kitchen. She, of course, began buzzing about, furious with me for calling her Silly Annie, but as usual, I ignored her complaints.

Once inside, I began to set up the clamp and funnel contraption that acted like a megaphone, so that her tiny voice was audible rather than the hissing and buzzing it amounted to without the device.

"Cyllene! See-lee-nee! Really, Siobhan, I think you mispronounce it just to annoy me," were the first words I could understand now that she had placed herself behind the pipe end of the funnel. *Well, of course I do it to annoy her.*

I opened the icebox and took out some vegetables to make a grab-it—a sandwich, in other words. You slapped your fillings between a couple of slices of bread and grabbed it with one hand. With all this sensory activity going on, I'd worked up quite an appetite! While fixing my grab-it, I began to tell Cyllene about my experience with the mysterious Dr. Wu.

"Everything about him is so vibrant. My fingers and toes never stopped tingling the whole time I was with him. His voice tastes like creamy butter on my lips and tongue. Although I could tell he had some cologne made up of chamomile and lavender, when he touched my hand, all I could smell was an exotic mixture of persimmon, plum, and pomegranate. He looks forty-something, but his eyes are much older than that, older than me or even you, I think."

Cyllene harrumphed at my reference to her being older than me, but she was, by a couple hundred years or so.

"Anyway, I was going to read his tea leaves, but he knocked the cup over, jostling the leaves. Though he apologized as if it were a mishap, I felt in my core that it was intentional. I pretended that the leaves were unable to reveal anything since they had been rearranged, but that wasn't true."

I hesitated, then shook off the shiver that ran down my spine as I remembered the image of the tea leaves.

"So? What did you see in the teacup?" Cyllene prodded me to continue.

"I saw an ancient temple or palace, kind of pagoda style. There was a boy. He was sick. I think he was dying. I am not sure how this connects to the young doctor, but I sense that it does. There was also something very dark and dangerous, but I couldn't make out exactly who or where it was coming from. All I know is that it feels so familiar to me! As if this is something I have been through before."

"Dark and dangerous!" Cyllene repeated, much more emphatically than I. "Oh, Siobhan, you must be careful around this man. Maybe he made the boy sick. One thing I'm sure about, your Dr. Wu is not who he seems to be."

"You might be right. I showed him the picture I had taken of the pendant that Mat is going to give Nina as a present. It is oriental in nature, and has Chinese-like characters inscribed around the rim of it. I thought maybe he could interpret it for me. He said it was an ancient script, and he wasn't too familiar with it, but again, I had my doubts about his veracity."

I bit into my grab-it, savoring the crunch of shredded carrots, sliced turnips, and arugula, and the tang of the vinegar and oil I sprinkled on it. My stomach rumbled back in appreciation. I gobbled up the rest of it quite quickly.

My hunger now sated and my story out of my head and off my lips, I felt much calmer. My sharpened senses had ratcheted down to a more normal level as the comfort of my own home sunk in, my closest confidante Cyllene by my side.

The thought of the *Wizards of the Orient* book popped into my head, and I was wondering just what kind of wizard this Timothy Wu might be. Maybe not the healing type, but maybe something more sinister. In my heart, for whatever reason, I hoped—prayed—not. Regardless, for the sake of Havenwood Falls and the universe itself, I needed to stay on my tippy toes, especially with everything going on. Maybe I'd better rethink that position with the school.

I finished my sandwich and offered Cyllene some peach nectar, which she declined. *Not a good sign. She's fading too fast.* I was getting ready to clean up the crumbs when Cyllene announced through her funnel-trumpet, "Don't bother, Siobhan. You have company!"

And sure enough, through the delivery slot in the back door hopped not one, not two, but all four pixie sisters. They tumbled to the floor through the slot, which only invited a pixie riot, also known as a wrestling match.

"Stop!" I hollered at them. *Just when I was getting my calm, cool, collected Celtic self back.*

Cyllene took charge at this moment. "Girls, there are some

wonderful grab-it crumbs available on the table and counter. Help yourself! I know all of you will clean up for Siobhan when you're done."

I let the pixie sisters know that there were also faerie cakes in the fridge if they were still hungry.

"I want one!" exclaimed Tierri, which was expected because she was always famished.

"Me too!" continued Enya, hopping on top of Tierri's shoulders, who was standing next to the fridge, and reached for the door handle.

"Me three!" shouted Ushka, followed of course by Aeiri with "Me four!"

Sometimes I wondered if these little sprites could count past four.

"I'm going to bed. It has been a very long day for me," I announced to my fae and forest friends, as I stretched out an overly pronounced yawn, hoping they got the hint to keep any racket down.

"Oooh, Siobhan, I almost forgot! I have something for you," Enya said, after she and her cohort in crime finished raiding the refrigerator. The little pixie reached into her nest of fiery red hair and pulled out a bit of lacy black ribbon.

"This is for you!"

"Well, thank you, Enya! It's lovely. And . . . black?"

"Yeah, isn't it cool? Nina gave it to me."

"Nina *gave* it to you?"

"No, really. She said I could have it. I didn't take it, really! She made this super cool wedding dress for Jetta Mills, with black lace and skulls, and it was a scrap she had left over."

"I remember seeing that wedding dress for Jetta. Even though it was black, she worked her magical tailoring talents for Jetta's happily ever after. Thank you for giving this to me, Enya."

Now I started yawning for real and couldn't stop. The pixie sisters were merrily nibbling away at the faerie cakes and grab-it crumbs, with Cyllene standing charge. She really made a great nanny for this brood.

I went up to my bedroom and opened the bureau drawer, pulling out my favorite flannel nightgown. Well, actually, all my flannel nightgowns were my favorite, but tonight I chose the dusty-blue one, because the color made me feel relaxed.

I crawled under my feather comforter and did my best to turn off the memories of my tea with the illustrious doctor, and wondering if the black ribbon may be some kind of omen.

CHAPTER 5

WU

I thought I was in luck last night with that tiny woman showing me the photo of the amulet, the very one I was looking for. The good news was that I had been right; the bad news was that it still eluded me.

So here I was, sitting at the Broastful Brew once again. However, I was astounded that this small establishment, in this far-fetched part of the world, whose purveyor was even more far-fetched, actually had Longjing tea. Unusual and . . . interesting.

The young bloke Madame Tahini had called her nephew Mat came to the table and asked me if I preferred my usual. I nodded politely at the boy and thanked him effusively for remembering. After all, I needed to engage him to get him to divulge the whereabouts of the amulet.

Mat brought me a very well prepared cup of Dragon's Well green tea, not quite as good as the last evening's, but after all, I brought my own Tiger Pond water to the mix yesterday.

"Mr. Mat," I started out. "That is your name, correct?"

"Yes, sir!"

"Please, call me Tim."

"Yes, sir . . . I mean, Tim."

"Your aunt, Madame Tahini . . ."

"Oh, you mean Siobhan. By the way, you have a markedly English accent for, well, someone from China. Well, at least, I'm told that's where you are from. Anyway, okay, a lot of folks around town call her Teeny Weeny Tahini, or Madame Tahini, but to me she's Aunt Siobhan. She may be tiny, but she's my superhero!"

He was young, but I was not too happy he caught on with the accent. On the flight over from China, once I took over this Tim Wu's body, I had the blessing to be placed between two very loquacious British gentlewomen, who not only chatted over me amongst themselves, but engaged me in conversation during the laborious twenty-plus hour flight. Apparently, I picked up their accent, but so far it seemed to be working well.

Siobhan . . . Well, that helps me in placing where she's from. I knew she wasn't from any area I was familiar with, but now it starts fitting together. Sounds Celtic or Gaelic.

"Your lovely aunt told me you had a lovely lady of your own," I said.

"Ah, yes, at least I hope so. Her name is Nina, and she is the best seamstress-slash-tailor in town. She just manages to work magic with cloth and textiles like you wouldn't believe! She's a superhero, too, in her own right!" The young man bragged on his woman.

"It sounds like you love and admire the woman. Have you asked her to marry you?"

"I want to in the worst way. But she's a bit skittish on the subject, and I definitely don't want to push her. The good news is I gave her a necklace last night. I was trying to hold out for a few more days, but I was too excited. She loved it! She said it gave her an unusual inspiration, especially for her next project."

Blimey. This poor young man was apparently greener than the tea I was drinking, telling me things I really had no right to know. However, it appeared I was once again thwarted in my quest to retrieve the amulet.

"So you say she is the best seamstress in town. I have a silk jacket that needs a bit of repair. Do you think I could take it to her?" I implored the fit young man.

"Absolutely! She's the only one you would ever want to take it to. Her shop is just around the corner, halfway down Eighth. There's a little alleyway, then her shop is on the second floor."

"Wonderful! I will take my jacket over there this morning."

"Well, that's probably not a good plan. Nina is a bit of a night owl, and unless she has a fitting appointment or something, she is not likely to open the shop before noon or even one o'clock. I can give you her card, and maybe you can set an appointment?"

This young Mat seemed very excited to garner some business for his beautiful talented tailor. Before I could even ask, he pulled a little card out of his pocket and placed it delicately by my teaspoon. He may have been green, but he had class, I must say.

I was not too happy that I had to wait a few more hours in the October chill that reminded me so much of the Wudang Mountains. I guessed I had no choice but to wander around the village for a while. I finished my tea, paid my bill, and as I exited out of the Broastful Brew, I pulled my afghan scarf closer around my neck to fend off the frosty breezes that seemed to come out of nowhere.

Knowing that the amulet was within my reach helped to inspire me and warmed me against some of the more ghastly, chilling elements here.

It was way too early to go to the lovely Nina's shop. I looked at the card the young man had given me. *Dress Perfect.* Since apparently I had a few hours to kill, I checked out the town square and familiarized myself with the territory.

I got to the center of town square, and there was a wonderful fountain flecked throughout with gold chips and flakes. There was a tourist couple also pondering the fountain. The wife was reading aloud from a "Welcome to Havenwood Falls" brochure.

"Henry, it says here that the gold traders donated to the town all the gold dust, flakes, and nuggets swept from their floors to make this fountain!"

The husband was not so gullible and told her he thought it sounded like some made-up story to impress the tourists.

But I sensed immediately that the fountain was indeed speckled with pure gold. One does not become an alchemist without feeling, smelling, and knowing gold. This was the real thing.

The couple moved on, brochure in hand, heading to the next point of interest. Apparently, it was the gazebo at the southeast corner of the park.

I stayed, staring into the glittering fountain, letting the energy of the gold fill me up. I'm not sure how long I stood there, entranced by its power, but when I came out of it, feeling fully recharged, the sun was much higher in the sky.

I scanned Main Street directly south of the fountain and saw a line of shops. Except the north end, where City Hall sat, all the streets around the square were lined with one- and two-story shops, it appeared. The one I noted, however, had a storefront window with mock Arabic lettering that read, *Madame Tahini's Potions, Lotions, Palm Readings, and Other Extra-Sensory Services.*

Well, there's a mouthful. So this is where the little fae works and lives. Yes, I was sure she was fae, not because of her small stature, but because she smelled fae. It almost oozed from her smooth, shiny skin and glowed from her flowing brown hair.

It was odd that her nephew had a slight scent of fae, but that was not his dominant nature. His smell was different, something of a mixture of forest and avian, but I just really couldn't fathom it. It seemed most everyone here smelled like something quite different than how they looked. Well, except for the mayor, other than being unusually tall and well-built, and that quirky little owner of the Broastful Brew. I was not sure what to expect from this Nina person, if indeed she was a human.

It finally began to warm up, and the rustling golden aspens quieted, indicating the breezes whipping through earlier had died down. I loosened my scarf and headed back to Whisper Falls Inn.

My little cottage was quite comfortable. I got the silk jacket out of the wardrobe and took a look at it. It was, of course, perfectly intact, but that wouldn't do at all. I got my straight razor from the bathroom and cut a few threads from the side seam of the jacket, then pulled the pieces of fabric apart to form a gaping hole. There was not too much damage, but certainly enough for the seamstress to repair.

Jacket in hand, I headed back to the center of town. I spotted a tavern on the corner of Eighth and Main and decided to get a refreshment before checking on the tailoring shop. What was it? Oh yes, Dress Perfect.

On my way to the tavern, I passed another coffee shop. This small town must love its coffee. I noted that, unlike the Broastful Brew, this coffee shop, Coffee Haven, appeared to be patronized by the younger generations of the town. A few teenagers in a booth by the front window pointed at me excitedly. I nodded and smiled and continued walking. *The kids these days are so uncouth.*

There it was, the Haven Saloon. Well, that name seemed appropriate. It even had frontier-like batwing doors to enter through. The place was dim, with bare wood rafters, and smelled of beer and what I would have normally said was wine, but there was a tinge of that sanguine scent, like what I sensed from that Michaela Petran.

There was a scruffy, rather scrawny middle-aged man, with a bandanna wrapped around his head, standing behind the bar. He greeted me as I entered, "Howdy, stranger!"

How quaint, how corny.

He took a toke from a fat joint, set it down in the ashtray, then waved his hand, welcoming me to take a seat at the bar. There were rows of wine bottles behind him, all with Stone Falls Winery labels and unusual names. For example: Wolf Pack Pinot Noir.

The glassy-eyed barkeep stuck his hand out to shake mine. "Name's Brent. The locals call me Bent Brent. What's your flavor, my man?"

"Well, by any chance might you have something in the way of plum wine?"

"Sure do! Make it myself every year. Teeny Weeny has a green thumb you've never seen the likes of, and gives me most of the damson plums from the tree in her backyard. You just stuff a big-ass glass jar full of those little beauties, add a bunch of sugar, fill it to the top with water, and of course some grain alcohol, then rotate it every day for a few months. Voila! Best plum wine ever!" And sure enough, he pulled a two-gallon glass jug from underneath the counter filled to the brim with a rich purple liquid. For a scrawny doped-up dude, his strength was impressive.

"Teeny Weeny?" I acted ignorant. *Teeny Weeny, now that really IS appropriate.*

"Oh, yeah, Madame Tahini, the itsy bitsy palm-reader down the street. She doesn't really drink, other than some whacked-up version of a virgin mojito, but we've been friends for a long time."

The wine was indeed good, just the right amount of acidic and sweet. Not a far cry from meijiu back home. I sipped it slowly, enjoying the astringent flavor of the wine.

"Well, my man, your plum wine is heavenly. You crushed it!" I tried using some of the words that kept popping in my head from the brain of the real Timothy Wu.

My new friend, Bent Brent, thanked me for the compliment and went back to his stogie. Hence the "Bent" part of his nickname, I supposed.

Savoring my last sip of this extraordinary plum wine, I glanced at the large clock made of a wagon wheel hanging on the back wall. At least ol' Bent Brent knew how to maintain a motif. It was nearly one o'clock, so I paid my bill, thanked Brent for the libation, placed my silk jacket over my arm, and headed out.

I crossed to the sidewalk at the south end of Eighth, and as I approached a small alley midway in the block, I saw a sign on the wall that read *Dress Perfect* with an arrow pointing upward, indicating the passage up the stairway in the alley toward the second floor flat. At the top of the stairs was a slender woman just entering into the shop. She had jet black hair, cropped short, revealing a long slender neck, and from my angle, I could see there was a gold chain hanging around it. I waited a few minutes before ascending the staircase, to give the seamstress a little time to situate herself.

As I entered the shop, the smell of rich espresso was prevalent. The young woman turned toward me, I believed a bit startled, but she recovered quickly. She was quite beautiful, with olive-toned skin and large dark almond-shaped eyes. And yes, she was wearing the amulet, but unfortunately, it was dangling from the dark side, once again.

"Are you Miss Nina?" I asked.

"Nina Messina, si. Buongiorno!" she replied.

I told her about the young chap from the coffee shop this morning who suggested I bring my jacket to her for repair and showed her the damaged article.

"I'm concerned because it is silk, but this young Mat insisted you were the best and could handle it."

"Si, I can do this, Mr. . . . ?" the young woman prodded.

"Dr. Wu, but please call me Tim."

"Ah, so you are the famous Dr. Wu everyone is talking about." She deftly took my jacket from my hands and placed it on a standing dress form.

"I should have this ready for you later this afternoon, about five?"

"That would be fantastic. I am much obliged. By the way, that's a stunning necklace you're wearing."

"Well, that young chap Mat you mentioned gave it to me, for a bit of an early anniversary gift."

"May I?" I said, at the same moment reaching for the amulet to turn it over. As I placed my hands on its rim, I heard a sudden searing sound, followed by the smell of burning flesh.

The young woman screamed out in pain, and I realized the amulet had melded into her skin. *What kind of curse is this? What's happening?*

She started backing away from me, clutching her chest, covering the pendant, or perhaps just in pain. I was not sure which, but I had to act fast. *I need that amulet!*

I grabbed the young woman by the nape of her neck, pulling out my vial of *dan*, and forcing her head backward, I poured the poisoning elixir down her throat. Immediately, she crumpled to the ground like a piece of one of her fabrics.

The mixture of cinnabar and mercury should have only caused a state like a temporary death, I hoped, but I needed time to figure out how to remove the amulet.

CHAPTER 6

TEENY WEENY

*T*he morning light streamed brightly through my bedroom window. It woke me up in a near panic. I never slept past the break of dawn. I looked at my cell phone, and it was nearly eight o'clock. I texted Barbie immediately to let her know I would be running late.

BS: No prob. Got paperwork. 9:30 ok?
TW: C U then
Hehe, I'm getting the hang of this.

I had so much to tell Barbie this morning, not only about my tea for two with Dr. Wu, but about the weird dream I had last night. Barbie, my go-to oneiromancer, would likely be able to interpret its meaning.

I was moving rather slowly, kind of all achy, but I guessed that was from a sensory overload from last evening's tea. It seemed to take me forever to just brush my teeth and wash my face. At the rate I was going, I felt I might actually need a cup of coffee this morning, just to get jump-started.

I did make it to the Broastful Brew by nine thirty, and of course I spotted Barbie at our usual table as I walked into the shop. The first thing I smelled was not coffee. It was that lavender and chamomile fragrance. I whipped my head around to see if Dr. Wu was in the Brew, but alas, all the tables except Barbie's were empty.

I didn't order coffee, of course. It's not my cup of tea. Mat was already coming over with the teapot, cup, and steeper before I could even sit down with Barbie. I was grateful the shop was otherwise empty.

"Mat, was Dr. Wu here this morning?" I asked my nephew, still bothered by the flowery aroma.

"Why, yes! He really likes that green tea that Mabel brews up for him. In fact, he was looking for a seamstress. Apparently, he has a silk jacket that needs mending, so I gave him Nina's card." He answered my question and then some. Poor boy, he just spilled his heart out.

Barbie grabbed my hand. "So . . . are you going to fill me in on your tea with Timothy?"

I basically reiterated what I told Cyllene the night before, though not quite in such detail, since I had already gotten the raw feelings off my chest by talking to the dryad. Then I told her I had a dream that maybe she could make sense of.

"Okay, hurry up. Let me hear about it." She eagerly invited me to share.

"I'm in some place very far away, in place and maybe even in time. There is a young boy lying on a large throne-like bed, dying. His parents are beside him, worried sick. The mother is doing everything in her power to keep from crying. The child is barely breathing, and it does not look like he has very much time left.

"The father came over to me and grabbed me by my shoulders, shaking me and hollering 'YOU MUST CURE HIM!'

"There is something about the color of the child's skin. He's not dying from an illness. I can see his veins through his nearly paper-thin waxy skin, and the veins are green. There is a smell about him too, something like five spice, but I'm not sure. One thing I am sure about —this child has been cursed.

"I sensed there is something special about this child. It seems that his parents are worried about something else too. Not just this child's fate, but something larger. The child has or had special powers. I could feel them surrounding me like a swirling light, but dimming fast and slowing down. My heartbeat almost came to a standstill when I touched him. Is he fae?

"I tell his parents that I believe there is a dark force responsible for his illness. I tell his parents that I need time . . . but really, I think I need my wand.

"Then I woke up."

Barbie took a long slow sip of coffee, uncharacteristically making a slurping sound in the process. "Hmm . . . Is this like your dream with your brother? Maybe it is a remembrance of something you've done before?"

"I wish. Then it would make some sense to me. I know it's been eons, but I don't have any recollection of anything like this. Does it have some alternate meaning? Or do you think the goddesses are trying to tell me something?"

"Ah, that could be it! Maybe they are trying to tell you to be a professor of Healing Arts at the college! Classes have already started, but you could come in for the spring semester." Barbie, bless her heart, was trying to use my dream to get her wish. Then again, maybe she had something there. "Don't worry, Siobhan. I'll think more on it and see if I can divine some inspiration for you." She patted my hand, finished her coffee, and bid me farewell.

Well, the day had gotten off to a late start, and I had plenty to do back home. I had a palm-reading appointment in the afternoon, and the had pixies devoured my stash of faerie cakes, so I needed to replenish my stock, and then of course Halloween was just around the corner. Hopefully, Mat and Nina would help again this year.

I waved goodbye to Mat and thanked Mabel for the tea as I headed back home to finish my chores and get ready for the couple coming in for their fortune-telling session, Henry and Grace.

Cyllene, of course, was waiting for me and floated in behind me as I entered the townhome and headed for the kitchen. I set up my beakers and flasks, pulled out a bowl and whisk, and searched the cupboard for the daisy flower flour.

While I was baking the third batch of faerie cakes and wondering if I should start on some pumpkin spice cookies, Nina dropped in for a brief moment on her way to work to show off the anniversary gift that Mat had given her last night.

Once Nina left, I realized there was a slight chill in the house, so I stoked a small fire in the fireplace to begin warming the place before my clients arrived.

Henry and Grace showed up at four o'clock sharp for their palm-reading, just as I finished placing the last of the faerie cakes on the cooling rack. I welcomed them in and led them to the salon. I noted the *Ancient Arts and Mystics* book was still on the table, and I grabbed it quickly and placed it on my chair.

An hour later, Grace was satisfied with her reading, and Henry the Unconvinced reluctantly pulled a few bills from his wallet. I left them with a blessing and hoped they enjoyed the rest of their visit in our lovely town. As I opened the door for them to exit, I saw the pixie sisters running down the block. I diverted Henry and Grace's attention to the clock on City Hall, and gave them some ridiculous story of how on Halloween the clock only ran backward, all of its own accord. While the couple was staring up at the clock, the imps ran underneath my legs and rolled into the foyer. Henry gave a harrumph at my outlandish tale, as I shrugged my shoulders and closed the door quickly behind them.

"Well, that was close! You gals need to be more careful. What's all the excitement about?" I asked the pixies, who were dusting off their knees and rabbit punching one another.

"We're going to apply to the College of Supernatural Guardians!" spouted Ushka.

"Are you now? And what makes you think you are qualified to go to college?" I asked.

"Well, we're supernatural!" Tierri stated matter-of-factly.

"Yeah, and we were your guardians in Gwynf'l, sort of, maybe, kinda, I think," Aeri said a bit skeptically while shaking her cloud-like white-and-pink locks about her head.

Hands on her hips, Enya insisted that they were smart, and they were going to write a story that would get them into the college.

"Really? Well, you are at least imaginative, I can admit that. Can you count to ten?"

"One!" cried Enya.

"Two," said Tierri.

"Three," added Ushka.

"Four," huffed Aeri.

Well, they got that far.

"Two!"

"Four!"

"Three!"

"One!" and back and forth between the four pixies, all the numbers out of order, continuing on for nearly ten rounds. *The closest they can get to the idea of ten, I guess.*

"See! We can count," Tierri exclaimed with a big grin on her face. "But we may need your help with the story, Siobhan."

"I can't help you write a story. You have to write your own story."

"We know, but we only know how to write in runes. We will need your help to translate it," Enya explained.

I grabbed some paper and pencils for the sprites and set them down in the living room, now pleasantly warm from the fire I started earlier. I left the sisters alone, saying a little prayer under my breath that this would keep them busy enough for me to clean up the kitchen and maybe have a nice quiet cup of chamomile tea. *Hmm . . . Maybe not chamomile tonight. That might be more stirring than calming.*

My tea brewed, I sat down at the small kitchen table, still clamped with Cyllene's megaphone, to take a sip when all four of the pixie sisters proudly strutted in, each with a sheet of paper in their hands, all waving them at me to look and read.

Enya and Tierri always seemed to take charge, so I took one of the sheets from Aeri, who was a bit shy to have hers read first, but handed it to me delicately.

The paper was full of rune-like figures—geometric shapes, wavy lines, a circle, a cross. These were indeed our ancestral runes. Aeri's read in English: *Fire 1 Earth 2 Air 4 Water 3*, and continued repeatedly throughout the page. I did not dare take her second sheet.

"Very nice, Aeri! Enya, let me see one of your pages." That of course did not take any cajoling whatsoever, as the imp slammed her paper down on the table proudly, triumphantly, and almost with an attitude that said, how dare I not choose hers first anyway.

Well, because in English it read like this: *Fire 1, Fire Fire 2, Fire Fire Fire 3, Fire Fire Fire Fire 4*

Not wanting to bore myself to death with reading all their pages, but trying to be supportive, I sent them back to the living room to compile their "story."

"You gals put your pages together, figure out what page is first, second, third, fourth, first . . ." *Jiminy criminy, I'm starting to sound like them.*

Fortunately for me, that's all it took. They delightedly threw all the pages into the air, each one grabbing another's, and off they rolled into the hearth room.

Ahh! I can finish my tea, maybe with a little peace and quiet.

BANG . . . BANG . . . BANG . . .

Holy junipers, WHAT THE HECK?

It was my door knocker, but never ever in my century and a half years here did it ever bang so loudly. Worse yet, I heard the etched oak door bang against the wall, and I knew intuitively that there would only be one person that would enter my home so boldly, and yet so humbly.

My poor dear nephew Mat charged into the foyer, nearly taking out the door frame with him. He was obviously distraught, to say the least.

"What's the matter, Mat?"

"Oh, Aunt Siobhan, I think Nina has stood me up. Maybe she's breaking up with me?" he responded in near tears.

"I highly doubt that, dear. What would make you think so?"

"She was supposed to meet me for dinner over an hour ago. I sat at the restaurant all that time waiting for her, but she never showed up, and she's not answering my calls or texts. Maybe the pendant I gave her wigged her out. If so, I'm glad it wasn't a ring."

"Mat, honey, Nina did not get 'wigged out' over your gift. In fact, she came by to show it off on her way to the dress shop this morning —well, actually, early afternoon. She loved it and told me how she was as happy the past two years as you. She's quite attached to the pendant."

"Oh. OH! Then she might be in trouble!"

I tried to calm this strong young man, now falling apart before my very eyes, and assured him we could find her. I sent him back to the restaurant, just in case she had the time wrong. Meanwhile, since I had a key to her shop, I told him I would go there to check it out.

"Maybe she fell asleep. I've caught her snoozing behind her bolts of fabric before," I informed Mat as we both headed out to search for Nina.

I checked in on the pixies before grabbing my wool coat and noted that they were now wrestling one another over whose pages went where. I called Cyllene into the living room to keep an eye on them, then rushed out the door. Something in the pit of my stomach told me Nina did not fall asleep.

I started to grapple for the key to the shop in my skirt pocket once I got to the top of the stairs at the end of the alley, but I saw the door was ajar.

"Nina? Yoohoo! Nina?" I called out, but no reply.

Nothing really seemed out of order, but there was a scent all mixed in with the usual espresso aroma that permeated Nina's shop. It was lavender and chamomile. *Again? Oh yes, Dr. Wu was supposed to see her.*

I noted the silk jacket Mat mentioned was still hanging on the dress form mannequin, and as I touched the jacket, an entirely different smell seeped into my nostrils. It was a metallic smell, part mercurial and what was that other thing . . . sulfur? The hairs raised up on my arms, telling me it was poisonous. This was a bad sign, I feared.

I texted Mat to meet me back at the salon, locked the door to the dress shop, and headed back home. Mat was already at the door waiting for me, and I suspected he had shifted into his owl self and flew back here to have arrived so quickly.

I raised my hand to place it gently on his shoulder—well, right below his shoulder, because I couldn't reach quite that high.

"I think Nina is with Dr. Wu," I tried to tell him calmly, especially since I didn't really have a lot to go on. *Dabbled in healing divination, my eye!*

Mat nodded. "She told me she heard about the town guest from the kids at Coffee Haven, where she gets her espresso. They were all excited about him being here, and she seemed just as excited, but then, that could have been the espresso talking."

"I think maybe it's not a good thing if she's with him. Now we need to find Dr. Wu, too. But at least I think I know where to find him. We need to go to Whisper Falls Inn. Stay here; I will be right back!"

I dashed into the townhome and scurried up to my bedroom. Grabbing the wooden box with the mysterious mother of pearl latch, I passed my hand over it, and the latch popped open. The wand nestled inside the case glowed dimly. *Just in case.* I wrapped my fingers around its shaft, lifting it out of its bedding carefully, then hurried back down the stairs to join Mat.

CHAPTER 7

WU

I waited until night had fallen to move the girl. My studies in the mystic arts had allowed me to master gravity and, in doing so, overcome it. It was a blessing for me this night.

As I exited the second-story flat, I scanned the surroundings and planned my escape route. I saw a snowy owl flying northeast, away from me. I didn't want anyone to see me, and though it was only a bird, I could not be sure in this town if it was indeed just a bird or something else—a familiar who may reveal my destination? A fae in disguise? I could take no chances.

Determining the coast was clear, the unconscious seamstress underneath my arm, so light and limp it was as if she were nothing more than a pillow, I leapt from the top landing of the staircase, across the alley to the top of the roof on the opposite side, and moved swiftly to the end of the row of shops. With the momentum of my run, I was able to jump catty-corner across the intersection. I continued swiftly across the roof of the Haven Saloon and westward toward Whisper Falls Inn, making a second leap across another alley, then once I was at the pawn shop, I took a deep breath, closed my eyes, and let my mind's eye soar me across Beaumont and Eleventh, where I moved stealthily, quietly to my cabin at the backside of the inn.

I gently placed the slumbering beauty on the bed in the back of the cabin and fetched my straight razor from the front room where I had left it after ripping my jacket open. I would use my surgical skills to remove the amulet that was now seared to her breast.

As I was about to make the first delicate slice between the amulet and the woman's skin, a piercing bolt of lightning flashed into my head, blinding me with pain. I heard the razor clatter to the floor as I regained my vision. *I have not had that happen since . . .*

Oh, divine spirit, thank you for your blessing and your protection! I had nearly forgotten in my haste that when one is under the influence of the Elixir of Immortality, a single drop of blood would destroy the spell and the soul would die. I could not have another death on my hands. I needed to come up with a different method to remove the amulet.

In the wardrobe was my black alchemist bag, and I fumbled through it to see if there was something among my mixtures, tinctures, and powders that would accomplish the task. Just as I was about to give up on this idea, my hand touched a small bottle. I could feel the tiny mosaic pieces that adorned it. It was my vial of Royal Water, what the Romans called *Aqua Regia*.

I pulled it out from the bag and held the bottle in front of me. The mix of acids that had been placed in this little glass jar, carefully lined in wax, held a precise three-to-one solution that would allow me to melt the gold from Miss Nina's chest without spilling a single drop of blood. It might burn her a little bit, but it appeared that had already happened to the unfortunate woman anyway.

I had to be careful with its application, though, as I could not take the risk that the script etched on the unrevealed side of the amulet melted in the process. I fumbled in the bag some more, as I was quite sure my glass straw was in there, and it would allow me to draw out the smallest amount of Royal Water from its special flask. My fingers identified the slender glass tube with its one end pinched so that only a tiny pinhole was present.

My index finger covering the wide end of the straw, I dipped the needle nose end into the vial of the caustic solution, then slowly I lifted my index finger to siphon up a small amount of the fluid. It was vital that I applied this sparingly around the rim of the amulet, so as not to destroy any of the engraving, but just to soften the metal enough to lift it from the lovely lady's chest.

I leaned over the sleeping beauty and cautiously, slowly allowed just the smallest amount of the liquid to drip upon the edge of the prized pendant, and continued to do so around its perimeter.

WHOOSH! WHOOSH! THUMP, THUMP, THUMP!

"Augh! It's too much! What was that?" The sudden noise coming from the living area startled me so that I lost my touch on the straw, and far too much of the liquid leaked on to the golden disk.

I quickly released the remainder of the fluid back into the vial and went to see what was the cause of all the commotion. But before I could even turn around, a sooty owl flew into the bedroom, swooping over my shoulder heading for the bedpost. My quick reflexes allowed me to grasp the creature's leg, and I swung it back through the door into the front room.

I heard the front door open, and realized Madame Tahini had just intruded.

CHAPTER 8

TEENY WEENY

*M*at shifted into his owl self and led the way to Dr. Wu's cottage, then disappeared momentarily before I saw him dive into the chimney of the cabin.

I ran as fast as my tiny feet could take me and attempted to charge into the cabin, but the door was locked. I could hear shuffling inside, a few squawks from Mat, then a loud thump and silence. I pointed my wand toward the door knob, letting its power overwhelm the lock, and the door flew open.

Mat was now a sooty grayish owl lying unconscious on the floor. Ash, soot, and feathers were drifting around the living area of the small cabin. But I saw no sign of the Wu. The door to the bedroom in the back of the cabin was open, and I could see Nina, but she was perfectly still, eyes closed and barely breathing.

I heard the front door slam shut as I rushed into the room, taking me by surprise, but I did not hesitate. As I entered the bedroom, I was struck from behind. I turned to see where the blow had come from but saw nothing. I scanned the room, and it was not until I looked up that I saw Dr. Wu crawling across the ceiling. I smelled melting flesh, and in a flash, I realized that the not-so-good doctor had been up to something very vile.

I pointed my wand at the man, and as I did so, the tip glowed brightly and a flash of electricity bolted from it. But the Wu was quicker and moved stealthily out of its way. He leapt from the ceiling in a midair somersault, landing directly in front of me. No sooner had he touched ground than his right foot took flight from the floor, connecting with my head in a painful blow.

I fell to the ground, but I kept a tight grip on my wand, which was a good thing, since I thought it protected me from any real injury the hit may have caused. I saw him once again running up the wall and across the ceiling, upside down. Again I pointed my wand in his direction, and again I missed the mark, as he did a double flip to the other wall. *Dang! I can't even do that!*

"You, little lady, are no match for me! Game on, sister!" He snickered as he said this.

"And you, Dr. Wu, are nothing more than a glorified alchemist, more of a sham than a shaman!" I shouted as I aimed my wand, this time with both hands on the shaft, and shouted as loud as I could, "*Wu Begone!*"

Several bolts of lightning flashed brilliantly from the wand's end, making the globe tip appear like one of those plasma balls the science nerds were so fascinated with. The strands of electricity surrounded the Asian man, trapping him like a giant claw and then knocking him to the ground.

He slowly got to his knees, and before I could take aim again, he pulled a small vial out of his pocket and threw it to the ground. The vial smashed into hundreds of tiny shards as a dense red smoke filled the entire room. I could barely see a dim glow from my wand right in front of me. My heart was pounding, but I could not give him a chance to hit me again, or worse, get a hold of the wand.

Tiny bubbles began to emerge from my skin, my fear and anxiety spinning them into motion far faster than usual, and I shrunk into my faerie form, looking much like a wispy fairy moth. My skin, hair, all of me, including my feathery wings and my wand, had gone completely white. This time it was I who flew up to the ceiling.

The smoke began to thin out, and I realized Mat had awoken from his stunned state, transformed into his human body, and opened the front door of the cabin, letting the red fog dissipate into the great outdoors.

I spied the shaman in the southeast corner of the room, moving nearer the napping Nina (at least I hoped she was just napping). He was searching the room, looking for me, unaware of my transformation.

"You cannot escape, Miss Teeny Weeny! This is *not* a game," he uttered, but this time without all the snickers. *Good, I think he's nervous.*

I was unsure of the energy of my wand in my faerie state. It was so small, and I was so new to its powers. I didn't want to give away my position, so I remained totally still, trying to think of a strategy.

The crimson fog was now only a thin veil, and I saw Mat grab the wizard by the nape of his neck, catching him totally off guard. Mat lifted him off the ground, but the Wu was swift, and with a chop of his hand to Mat's wrist, the grip was lost. The Wu spun out of his way and onto the northwest wall, swiftly climbing to the top. It was from that vantage point that he spied me directly diagonal from him.

I could see for a moment he was not sure if I was just an unsuspecting insect that had accidentally flown into the situation or something else. But that moment vanished in an instant as he realized that it was me in the opposite corner.

He reached into his pocket again, pulling out yet another vial. So much for strategy. I didn't have time to come up with something fearsome or clever, not with both Mat and Nina at risk too. Clinging to the ceiling with my wings pressed to the rafter, I aimed my now tiny wand at the Wu and whispered softly, "*Wu Begone.*"

The sensational streaks of electricity that occurred previously did not appear this time. Instead, a stream of silky threads spewed from the glowing orb at the top end of the shaft, and within seconds, the wonderful wizard of Wu was trapped in a spider web in the far corner of the room, along with his vile vial.

I took another shot at the shaman, adding a second layer of the webbing. *Just in case!*

Mat was standing over Nina, wringing his hands, deep crevices of concern appearing on his brow. There was dripping gold and flesh on Nina's chest, although most of the pendant had retained its shape. He reminded me of the worried people in that dream with the dying young boy.

I effervesced back into my human glamour, the bubbles now becoming rainbow colors rising from my form as the paleness of my fae faded away and the colors of this world returned to my skin and hair.

"What have you done, Wu? Why are trying to kill Nina?" I interrogated the imprisoned imposter.

The webbing was now so thick that Tim Wu could only mumble as the threads of the web tightened their hold upon the struggling sorcerer.

At that moment my cell phone vibrated, and I pulled it from my pocket to see a text from Barbie.

BS: Not U! It's Wu!

What the heck does that mean? I punched her little avatar above the message and let the phone dial her directly.

"Barbie, what does this message mean? I have Wu trapped here in his cabin. He kidnapped Nina, and I don't know what he's done to her. Maybe you need to bring Sheriff Kasun here."

"Siobhan, your dream! That's not you in the dream. That's Dr. Wu who was ordered to cure. It was in the tea leaves you told me about. I'll be there in just a few minutes. If we need to, we'll call the sheriff later. Just keep Dr. Wu busy for now."

No worries! I plan to keep Dr. Wu tied up for some time.

I joined Mat by the bedside to evaluate Nina's condition. Like the boy in the dream, her skin was becoming waxen and pale as she drew weak breaths erratically and too far apart for comfort.

I returned to the Wu and cautiously pointed my wand at the area in the web where the mumbles seemed to be coming from. A delicate glow emitted, and a small circle burned through the webbing where the doctor's mouth would be.

"Again! Why are you trying to kill Nina?" I pressed him.

Barbie entered the cabin just in time to hear this villain's lame excuse.

"Madame Tahini, I am *not* trying to kill Nina! I am a healer, not a killer! But we must act fast, or else the *dan* may take over, and she may not be able return to our world. You must set me free now!"

"How can I trust you?" I screamed at him. This took me by surprise, and I jumped at the sound of my own voice. "You are a deceitful devil, a shamming shaman, a wicked wizard, a mean magus, a pathetic parasite . . ." I ran out of awful things I could throw at this atrocious alchemist . . . "Oh yeah, and an atrocious alchemist!" I added.

Barbie cut in, and in her officious demeanor, questioned him. "Dr. Wu? Who are you? Really?"

She asked this with such fierceness of authority that even I felt like there was something I had to confess.

"Madame Mayor, I am Tang Wu from the Zhou Dynasty. I am the Master Wu for the royal family. Their son, a young boy, has been gifted by the spirits with special powers that will heal and protect the people of the kingdom, and in fact, the world. But he is dying. A significant evil, determined to destroy the mysteries, mystics, and spirits, has placed a curse on him. I was ordered to cure him, but the only antidote, the spell that will break the curse, is on the other side of *that* amulet. I have failed, and to that end, I know not what will happen to your world, if mine becomes extinct."

I could feel the anguish and heartache in his voice, and it cut me to the core. That tingling sensation in my fingertips and toes began again. I didn't know what to make of it. The truth of his words spun twinkling stars in my head.

"If we can get you the amulet, will Nina be okay?" I beseeched him.

"I can only hope I have not ruined the amulet when I used a Royal Water solution to solve the problem of removing it. But, yes, your Nina should be revivable," he replied woefully.

"Should be? I'm afraid, Dr. Wu, that is not good enough!" Mayor Barbie stated matter-of-factly. "If she does not revive, you have a very serious charge against you and you will face the Court! You will be facing the Court nevertheless, since you failed to inform us of your powers for the Registry."

"The pendant has a protective spell on it. Only Nina's true love can remove it," I began to explain, and looked at Mat still standing beside Nina's prone body with a questioning look.

"I don't know, Aunt Siobhan. She is my true love, but I cannot say that I am hers. What if I make it worse and embed the pendant even deeper into her?" he responded.

"You have been with Nina for two years. As the blessing says, time will tell. Remove the amulet, Mat," I gently commanded my dear lovesick nephew.

His large hands shaking, he stretched his fingers around the circle of the amulet. Nervously, he touched its rim.

CHAPTER 9

TEENY WEENY

*W*e all kept perfectly still as Mat gently attempted to lift the pendant from Nina's chest. It began to glow with a golden light around its entire circumference. With his eyes squeezed shut, too fearful to see if he might be causing his love any injury, he lifted the coveted charm from her chest with ease.

I took the amulet from his hand as he gave a heavy sigh of relief and sat down on the bed beside Nina, who was still in a deep state of slumber, or whatever it was the Wu had placed her in. The amulet was now safe, albeit not sure how sound it was, as it appeared to have suffered some damage from Wu's so-called solution.

Nina, however, had not come to. She was still in her restful repose, and it was clear that it was Wu's elixir that kept her in this state, and not the necklace that had adorned her. I was relieved that it was not something I'd done with the protective spell I'd placed on the piece of jewelry. Then again, since Mat was able to remove it from her neck, if it had been part of the spell, Nina would be back with the living.

"Well, Mr. Tang Wu, what do you propose to do to revive her?" I implored him.

"I can do nothing if you don't release me from this web!" he replied.

I was just about to unravel the silky cocoon still containing the mysterious Wu when Barbie stopped me.

"Siobhan, let me call Sheriff Kasun over now. We don't want any surprises without him standing by." She took her cell phone out of her purse and punched in a direct code for the sheriff. Explaining the situation briefly, she asked him to get to the cottage as soon as possible.

Aside from the fact that the town was relatively small, it was still a wonderment that the supernaturals could move so quickly, and the sheriff's "as soon as possible" was almost instantaneous, utilizing his wolf's swiftness.

I gave the sheriff a quick rundown of the battle that had ensued between the Wu and me, which led him to his current imprisoned position. The sheriff nodded, understanding the danger, and placed his hand on his holster, not inconspicuously, even though I doubted the wizard was able to see his movement through the thick gauze that enshrouded him.

I twirled my wand around the exterior of the wrapped Wu, allowing the silken threads to disintegrate, freeing the master.

Tang Wu began to move toward the closet, but the sheriff grabbed him by the shoulder, stopping him in his tracks.

"I need my bag in order to prepare the Elixir of Life. That is the only thing that will revive the young woman. Hopefully, it is not too late, as it is nearly midnight and the stars will align themselves in a way that may make it impossible for her to come back," he explained.

"Come back? Come back from where?" I asked, my voice now edged with heightened anxiety.

"She is entranced with the Elixir of Immortality. It allows the subject to enter a higher plane, a plane of enlightenment. It causes a temporary death, so to speak, as her soul enters this elevated level. The timing is essential to administer the Elixir of Life, which will return her soul back to this plane. If she is too long in the temporary death and the stars realign, the cord between the two planes will be broken."

Mat held up a black medicine bag that he had garnered from the closet while Mr. Wu gave his dissertation.

"Is this it?" he asked.

"Yes, quickly, bring it here."

The sheriff maintained his grip on the shaman's shoulder as Mat placed the bag at his feet. Wu rustled around in his bag and took out a copper vial and a blue silk bag embroidered with a white crane and multi-color starbursts, then cinched closed with a red braided string. He also removed a small wok-shaped bowl and placed it on the floor. The master wizard opened the bag and poured a pinch or so of purplish flakes into the bowl, then with an eyedropper, he withdrew a brownish liquid from the copper container and added it to the mixture. It began to bubble immediately as the chemicals interacted with one another, the flake mixture dissolving, and a violet plume arose from the simmering stew. Within a few moments, the bubbling had ceased, and the Wu once again used the eyedropper to withdraw a portion of the mixture from the bowl.

The sheriff did not trust the Asian stranger, especially now, knowing that there was an attack on one of Havenwood Falls' oldest citizens, and refused to let the man budge. I took the eyedropper from his hand and went to Nina's bedside. I gently placed the open end of the dropper on her lips, letting the small tube part them somewhat. As the City Hall clock tower began to strike its midnight toll, I released the liquid into her mouth and held my breath, just as it seemed Nina had been holding hers for the past few hours. I could sense that everyone in the room had ceased to breathe for the entire tolling of the twelve chimes.

On the last ring of the clock tower, a cumulative exhale came from all except Nina. It appeared that Tang Wu's potion either did not do the trick or we were indeed too late administering the antidote.

Mat began to cry.

"Nina, Nina, Nina. Please come back! I am your true love, and you are mine. You must be in this world!" Then he pressed his lips to Nina's just as the echo of the twelfth bell dwindled into infinity.

Sheriff Kasun was unfastening his cuffs from his belt when a loud gasp shattered Mat's cries, and Nina's eyelids fluttered, then opened slowly, her eyes drowsily taking in the wet-cheeked Mathieu. She lifted a weak hand to his cheek and uttered, "Ciao, mi amor. What are you doing here?"

Clearly, Nina had not yet realized that she was back in our world, but that mattered not to Mat, who wrapped his large arms around the lithe frame of the Italian seamstress, seeming like he might knock the wind right out of her again. But like his love for her, the hug was gentle and kind.

Interrupting the lovers' display of affection, Barbie requested the sheriff put Dr. Timothy Wu or Master Tang Wu, or whatever his name was, into the lockup.

Tang begged me to hand over the amulet, but I refused. It would remain in my safekeeping for now, and we would discuss it tomorrow in front of the Court of the Sun and the Moon. Tang Wu looked miserable, and that made me happy, but not really. I suspected we would all be more enlightened come tomorrow.

CHAPTER 10

WU

The bars on the cell they placed me in were obviously more than just a physical barrier. There seemed to be some spell placed on them, since I couldn't even use my mind-bending to budge them. Or perhaps it was just me. After all, it had been a long night, I was still no closer to accomplishing my task, and I was so weary.

Hmm, that little fae had some big power. I had underestimated her. In fact, I thought, I had underestimated her in more ways than one. She seemed to affect me in a way that I could not really fathom. There was something about her that made me feel I needed to have her close by. I certainly hoped she would forgive me for the wallop I gave her, but I had a duty to perform. Even though I was a total failure.

The overhead lights in the jail cell kept the area brightly lit, but I was the only prisoner this evening, which was just as well. It would give me some solitude to call on my spirit.

I knelt in a corner of the cell facing the wall opposite the bars, imagining there was a window near the ceiling. Closing my eyes, I envisioned the moon shining brightly amongst a sea of glittering stars, then cleared my mind and began my divination chant.

"Qǐzhòngjī, mighty spirit. Wings of Wisdom, Feathers of Faith."

I repeated this chant over and over again until my head began to swirl and my body was lifted from the ground. I floated in midair in the center of the cell, enveloped by the velvety darkness of the night and surrounded by the twinkling stars—at least in my mind. My glorious Spirit Crane flew in and made a circular flight around my body before landing. As she did so, the crane's body transformed, melding into the shape of a tall, lean woman whose skin and robe were completely white. My floating body declined back to the floor, and I arose. She stood before me, her right leg bent with her right foot propped on the other leg, in a crane's stance.

This is my divining spirit the great Qǐzhòngjī, the great white Crane. She is my protector and my healer, my spirit teacher and my guide.

As I looked at her now, in her non-celestial form, I noted she looked remarkably like Madame Tahini in her fae form, the one I spotted right before she pointed her tiny wand my way and wrapped me in a web. Perhaps this might have something to do with why the little woman affected me so much.

"Tang Wu, loyal servant, how may I assist you?" the crane-woman prodded me gently.

"I have been set with the task of curing the young prince, but rather it is more un-cursing than curing that is needed, Mighty One. There is an amulet that holds the spell to break the curse, and I have tracked it to this place. In fact, I nearly had it in my hands, but I am thwarted at every turn. There is magic and mystery abounding here, but it is beyond me, Great Spirit."

"Ah, Tang Wu, you are here because it is part of your journey. You will need to draw from the strengths you learn here to help the Zhou prince of your past."

"Great Crane, I thank you for your wisdom." I bowed my head in a grateful gesture and continued, "I am also confused about a woman who has been involved with the amulet, a spell that protected it, and a wand that has more power than I have ever seen."

"Tang Wu, I sense in your voice that your confusion is more than just her spells and wand. I sense she has a power over you. I will grant her blessings this night, and in the daylight, perhaps both of you will see clearer."

"Again, I thank you for your wisdom and the blessings you

bestow." I bowed again before the Great Spirit, this time all the way to the floor in total servitude. She placed her soft hand upon my forehead, and I could feel that she was gleaning my thoughts and memories. As she did this, she transformed once again into the mighty white crane, and her hand became her wing. She took flight, circling above me and out of the channel, taking the stars and the velveteen night sky with her. I was left once again in the glaring light of the jail.

I wondered what blessing the Great Spirit Crane would bestow upon Teeny Weeny. I prayed that it would be forgiveness.

CHAPTER 11

TEENY WEENY

J had a fitful night's sleep with so many things dancing in and out of my head all night long. I must've awoken at least twelve times during the night. It was almost like my brain was tolling the stroke of midnight, but every half hour.

Cranes invaded my dreams constantly, and that was bewildering. Great white flying birds, with brilliant moon beams spraying off their downy wings. Cranes watering at a shining aquamarine pond, not so dissimilar to our own Peacock Lake at Smalls Falls. The pond lay in front of a pagoda-type building. It seemed Master Tang Wu and his little bag of tricks left an indelible impression.

His face kept swimming in and out of my dreamy head during the sleepy/sleepless night, but it wasn't always the face we had seen this past week. At times it was an older face, with gentle lines creasing his forehead, a long flowing white Fu Manchu mustache melding into a goatee made up of silken threads like those I had entrapped him in, and soft dark almond-shaped eyes that seemed to glimmer with love and hope.

I found these two contrasting visions of Wu very disturbing. Then there was the vision of him running up walls and across ceilings, doing somersaults in midair, with colorful smoke fading in and out of the picture.

Every time the vision of the older Wu came waffling into my head, my fingers and toes wriggled with that funky tingling sensation I had experienced so many times in the doctor's presence.

I supposed doctor was appropriate. Although he was a wizard in its most explicit terms, he did far more than just dabble in divination and play with potions. He obviously knew not only his alchemy but herbs, elements, spirits, spells, and healing ointments.

And speaking of elements, there was something elementary about the effect he seemed to have on me, regardless of our differences, battling or otherwise.

After about six hours of non-sleep, I gave up and got out of bed. I was exhausted, apprehensive, excited and concerned, mostly about the assembly at the Court, but also about seeing Timothy/Tang Wu. I was looking forward to seeing the Master Wu and didn't really know why. I was definitely in need of a strong cup of chamomile tea this morning to calm my nerves. *I'm almost thinking that a touch of lavender might not be a bad idea either. Then again, maybe NOT.*

I padded my way down the stairs and into the kitchen that doubled as a laboratory at the back of my townhome. Cyllene was already by the windowsill. I set the kettle on the stove, opened the window just a smidge to allow my dear friend to waft in, and closed it quickly behind her, as the late October chill was still present this early.

Like an automaton, I instinctually set up her funnel and clamp contraption so that we could converse.

"Siobhan! Where have you been? Why do you look so, well, so tired?"

"Ah, Silly Annie, it was a long night, and I did not get to bed until after midnight."

"Midnight! You can't stay up later than eight o'clock, or sundown even, depending which comes first!"

Well, actually she was right. She'd known me for over a hundred years, and that had not changed, other than of course, the changes that seemed to keep occurring since Mat arrived more than two years ago. *Or maybe it IS something else?*

Cyllene deserved an explanation, and I proceeded to tell her about the adventures of yesterday—the disappearance of Nina (she gasped), Mat's flight down the chimney (she gasped), Nina's coma (she gasped), and my battle with Dr. Wu (she double gasped). At this point, I had to slow down, as I was not really sure how much gasping a poor little dryad could take.

I finished brewing my tea and went over to the small kitchen table where Cyllene and her "microphone" were set up. But when I looked at her, she was not the same sunset moth-styled dryad with whom I was familiar. She looked almost like a white crane, and I was so taken aback, I spilled my tea and knocked over my chair.

I righted the chair and cleaned up the spilt mess from the floor. *Maybe I should pay attention to my own tea leaves.* I sat down, trying not to stare at this miniature white crane. But the tiny white bird wasn't there. Cyllene was exactly that—Cyllene.

"Siobhan! Are you okay?" came her lilting voice from the wide end of the funnel.

"For just a second, you looked like something else, like a bird—a crane to be exact. I guess my mind is playing tricks on me. Probably due to the restless night's sleep I had."

"Restless night?"

I continued with my story while brewing another cup of tea, since my last cup wound up on the floor. I told her about wrapping up Dr. Wu in a cocoon, the sheriff's arrival, Wu mixing the Elixir of Life from the flakes he shook out from the mysterious little crane-embroidered bag, Mat kissing Nina, and the sheriff taking the wizard off to jail. I took a deep breath and sat down with a fresh cup of steaming chamomile tea while Cyllene was absorbing my words.

"After I got home and went to bed, I kept having visions of Wu, cranes, and all sorts of strange places. I'd fall asleep briefly, and then another apparition would wander into my head. It appears I will need to do a little research before we assemble at the Court. I've got the amulet now, but I don't know how damaged it is, or how exactly it plays into this scenario. I also need to see if I can find some information about what the crane symbolizes. I know it's linked to Wu somehow."

I got up from the table and was headed toward the salon when my cell phone vibrated in my pocket. I took a look, and it was a message from Mat.

MM: Nina has this scar now. Is there something you can do for it?

A picture of Nina's emblazoned chest followed the text. The pendant that had seared itself to her chest when Wu tried to take it had left an imprint of the design on her skin. The photo showed her skin a bit reddened, but it did not seem too serious.

TW: will chk HOHUM & get back 2 u. Any pain?

Yeah, I got this.

MM: She said no.

I knew my *Handbook of Healing Unctions and Mixtures* (HOHUM) should have just the right recipe to heal Nina's scar. So I added this to my research list and continued into the salon and my extensive library of spellbound books. Of course, they were not really spellbound, but they were bound, and most contained spells, so there you had it.

I kept HOHUM fairly handy, as healing was my nature and the reason why my backyard garden was so thick with herbs, plants, and fruit trees. I placed the manual on the round table that sat in the center of the salon, next to *Ancient Arts and Mystics,* which I had left out earlier in the week.

I thumbed to the index to search for *crane,* and no surprise, it led me back to the chapter on "Wizards of the Orient." I continued where I left off the last time, and it read:

"The Wizards of the Orient typically use spirit divination in their arts and practices. They align themselves with one of the spirits, such as the Spirit Turtle, Spirit Dragon, and Spirit Crane. *See additional reference material: Spirits & Totems.*"

Ah, it just so happened I had that book! It was on a lower shelf of my wall of books, so I did not need the ladder. I pulled it out and again placed it on the table and searched through the index for *crane.*

I found the page on Spirit Crane and read:

"The Spirit Crane totem represents longevity and the creative connection with the eternal and divine. When a crane totem appears, it means that you need to use the power and strength from the past to deal with the present. The specific crane denotes specific attributes.

"The white crane symbolizes faithfulness and wisdom. It is one of the most powerful healing spirits in the oriental arts."

Well, that certainly explained a lot. This Spirit Crane was obviously connected to Wu. He must use its divination to achieve his goals. Since cranes appeared to me last night, I needed to keep in mind that I would have to use my past strengths—*my wand?*—to deal with him now.

Next I looked to see what HOHUM had for Nina's wound.

It didn't take very long to find the right recipe for the salve that would heal her scar and rejuvenate her skin to its original silky smoothness. But of course the recipe called for chamomile and lavender, however, this time mixed with the milk from dandelion stems, all of which I had in abundance in my garden. *Darned dandelions. Well, in this case, darling dandelions.*

I took a look at the amulet now. I had been apprehensive to look at it since last night's episode. The side with the colorful yin yang was indeed damaged. There were parts around the rim where the Chinese characters were blurred and one or two were totally obliterated. If the Wu did indeed need the spell on this charm, I was afraid it wouldn't be of much help now. Nevertheless, I planned on taking it to the Court, and maybe he could make something out of it.

CHAPTER 12

TEENY WEENY

I dressed as quickly as I could; time was running short before I had to be at the Court. I was so nervous that I had trouble just pulling a skirt on. I took a linen handkerchief from the bureau drawer and placed the pendant in the middle of it, then wrapped it carefully before placing it in the pocket of the skirt I finally managed get on. I grabbed a thick pullover sweater, since buttons were out of the question this morning, and a thick wool scarf, as the weather was getting colder day by day.

Once downstairs, I pulled on a pair of fleece-lined Sherpa boots and a down sleeveless vest. I remembered Cyllene was still hanging out in the kitchen, so I ran in to open the window so she could flit out and join her beloved tree Maximus. Thankfully, no pixies visited this morning.

I hurried out the front door, locking it behind me, then crossed Main Street and the square to get to City Hall. I of course did not go through the front door. I headed around to the back of City Hall, double checking to make sure no one noticed me, to a most unobtrusive looking entrance to the Court—a large metal door that looked like a maintenance door, except there was a relief of a moon and a mountain hammered into it.

I pulled the heavy door open, went down a flight of stairs, then through the long hallway before entering into the large courtroom. A few small rows of seats made up the gallery that faced a large wood-paneled dais. In front of the gallery was a table and a single chair—that would be the "hot seat."

I noted that all the chairs behind the table on the dais were occupied, except of course mine. I bade good morning to each of the Court members assembled for the emergency meeting—Michaela Petran, Saundra Beaumont, Roman Bishop, Barbie Stuart, and the rest of the cast—as I scampered past them toward the last chair on the panel and took my place.

Sheriff Ric Kasun was standing in the back of the room, waiting for the signal. Roman banged a gavel, alerting the Court members that the session had now begun. Mayor Barbie nodded at the sheriff, who opened a door in the back of the courtroom, and Ric's deputy escorted Dr. Timothy Wu—now known to most of us as Tang Wu—hands cuffed behind his back, to the hot seat.

The sheriff recited from his notebook the events of yesterevening that led to the wizard's arrest. The Court members were intrigued, and a few of them even looked over at me, nodding their condolences or giving me an admiring smile. They certainly were not used to me defending myself, but then I'd rarely been in a position to do so, other than the episodes with the she-cat Shayin Pisik.

After the sheriff finished reading his notes, Roman Bishop nodded at Barbie. She cleared her throat and began to speak.

"Sir, you are before this Court not only on the charges that the sheriff has just described, which include but are not limited to putting one of our citizens in an induced coma that practically killed her and attacking one of our oldest and dearest Court members, Teeny Weeny Tahini. But you, sir, deceived the Court by pretending that you were the famed Dr. Timothy Wu, when in fact you are a wizard, an alchemist to boot. That is something you failed to inform the Court, let alone register with us. What do you have to say in your defense?"

"Madame Mayor, let me first start off by apologizing to the entire Court. When you offered the invitation to the prominent Dr. Wu, it was the opportunity I needed to find the amulet that will save my kingdom and the world as you know it. Timothy Wu is a descendant of mine. That is why I am able to inhabit his body. I had already tracked the amulet down to this place, Havenwood Falls, and this time. It was just a matter of getting here.

"I am on a mission. My emperor's son is dying. As I told you before, I am from the Zhou Dynasty. The young prince was blessed by all the spirits with a special gift, one of love and compassion that transcends our normal understanding of such things. He was destined to rule the dynasty and keep intact the teachings and healings of the spirits so that the mysteries and magic of the universe would not be destroyed. But there is something viciously evil in my time, and perhaps even yours, that placed a curse on the young boy. This curse is inscribed on an amulet, as the spell that can break the curse is inscribed on its opposite side.

"The amulet is the very reason I am here, because it is. The young woman Nina, who was simply the unfortunate recipient of a gift, was wearing it, and as I went to examine it, the amulet became nearly surgically attached to the poor girl. I believe a protective spell must have been placed upon it for something like that to happen. Unfortunately, the exposed side of the amulet is the curse, which I already know too well.

"If my young prince dies, there is a chance that the evil that is trying to destroy the mystery and magic of the world will succeed, and then even Havenwood Falls may not exist as you know it. All of you, in fact, may cease to exist. It is a paramount mission, and I appear to be failing at it miserably.

"Truly, I intended no harm, but I was at a desperate point and was at odds on how to solve it."

Mr. Wu bowed his head and added, "Madame Tahini, I hope you can forgive me, most of all."

He could not even look me in the eye when he said this, but I was glad he didn't, because I might have fallen apart right on the spot. First, because it was I who placed the protection on the pendant in the first place, and second, because I was afraid I would have seen the truth, despair, and caring in Wu's eyes as I heard it in his voice.

Barbie asked me if there was anything I wished to contribute to this tribunal. I stood and reached into my pocket, pulling out the kerchief-wrapped charm. I motioned to the sheriff to take it and show it to our defendant.

"Mr. Wu," I started, "is this the amulet?"

"Yes, the very one. It is thousands of years old."

"And the inscription you are seeking? Is it of any help?"

I was hoping for his sake that it was not too damaged to decipher, but as he turned it over, his face was crestfallen, and I knew that it did not reveal all that he needed to break the damned curse.

"I'm afraid, Madame, that I continue to fail, as I am the one who caused this damage. The essential elements of the spell are too obscured to make out." His disappointment and pain were loud and clear. I remembered feeling that kind of pain when my father had cursed my brother Grenfold, and I felt I could do nothing to stop it.

"Your Honors," he addressed the entire court, "do with me what you will, as I am no good to my people. My emperor has already warned me that if I cannot cure the prince, I will be executed. And I am surely no good to your people, as I have already hurt some of them."

I heard Barbie and Roman whispering, then the others chattering back and forth. I wondered if they would send him back to his own time to be beheaded or whatever they did there. His infractions here were not so serious as to warrant execution.

Roman once again banged the gavel. The Court members shushed each other, and the room fell silent.

Barbie ordered the Wu to stand while she laid down the law and pronounced his sentence.

"Mr. Wu," she began again, "though we sympathize with your predicament, the Court feels it is best that you be returned to your original home in your original time. We anticipate that you will cooperate with the Court so that they can make the appropriate preparations to send you back."

The agonizing doctor simply nodded his acquiescence. My stomach became a leaping frog, bouncing up into my throat and back down. The tingling in my fingers and toes became a violent burning. My head was pounding so furiously with the sound of rushing blood, as if every vein in my brain had become a rogue wave. I felt I was about to vomit, but then my cell phone vibrated. *Oh my gods and goddesses! The phone, the photo, the pendant, it's all here, all clear.*

"WAIT!" I shouted out so uncharacteristically that Lilith Blackstone and Mathilde Augustine were startled out of their seats.

"Siobhan?" the mayor addressed me. "You have something to say?"

"I have a picture of the amulet. It's on my phone! I mean the right side of it, truly the *right* side. The one with the spell that could break the curse." I pulled out my phone and opened the photo that Mat had sent me this morning. I got up from the dais and walked the phone over to Tang Wu. This was probably dangerously close, considering how he made me feel, but I felt I must try to save him.

For a brief moment, a flash of hope fleeted across his features, but then he looked at the picture on my phone, the one of the imprint in Nina's skin, with all of its intricacies and delicacies. Alas, he shook his head once again in dismay and what I sensed was frustration.

"What? What is it? What's wrong?" I begged him.

"It doesn't make any sense. The characters are all wrong. It's unintelligible. Even the yin yang is backwards!"

"It is? The yin yang is backwards? Is that even possible? Wait! This is a picture of the amulet emblazoned on Nina, of course it's backwards! Really we should say reversed."

Ric Kasun came to my rescue, taking the phone from my trembling hand. He downloaded the picture into my photo album, then played around with some of the tools in the app and managed to flip the photo. He posed the phone in front of the master, and joy lit up his face. For a moment, I saw the true face of Tang Wu—his white hair, his wizened skin, his beautifully compassionate eyes—the face that appeared in and out last night.

"That's it! That is the cure, the spell! I must study this and be sure that I have it right before I return. Your Honors, please give me a little more time here before returning me to the Zhou Dynasty. I'll register. Whatever it takes!"

Roman looked at me and at Barbie, then at the other members of the Court. They all seemed to be in congruence for a change, except maybe Lawrence Mills, who could often be a bit of a curmudgeon, but even his nod came.

"Mr. Wu," Barbie once again laid down the law, "we will give you four days. You will register immediately after this meeting with Adelaide Beaumont, and you will be under house arrest until the end of your four days. You will work with Siobhan, that is Madame Tahini, to discern this spell, and anyone else she feels may be necessary to assist. And you will cooperate fully!"

Roman Bishop banged his gavel once more, and spoke for the first time, which was unusual to say the least. "Dismissed."

CHAPTER 13

TEENY WEENY

I was so excited that Tang would not be executed. I mean relieved, of course. I was happy that he would be here for at least a few more days. I was terrified that he would be here for at least a few more days. *Sheesh, I'm so conflicted!*

The Court disassembled, and as I headed back to my townhome, I remembered the cell phone had vibrated while we were in session. I checked my messages again, and of course it was from Mat. He was only asking again about Nina's scar. I had completely forgotten to let him know that I found the right recipe for an ointment that would not only help the scar, but that she might want to use religiously, all over her body, and he may want her to too, since it was like an anti-aging cream.

TW: Yes got it! B ready by 4

As soon as I got home, I headed to the back of my house and out the back door from the kitchen that led into my garden, grabbing my snippers from the counter on my way out. I had to push back a few blackberry brambles, as they had taken over most of the walkway all on their own. We had already experienced a bit of snow, but a little fae magic and a touch of Addie's helping witchcraft went a long way. The garden was still bright and green, and yes, overflowing with dandelion weeds.

This day, I was grateful. The fronds of lavender protruded every which way they chose, but there were plenty. The backyard was so overgrown, I had to rack my brain to remember where the chamomile was planted, or had chosen to plant themselves was more likely. *Oh! There they are, right next to a great patch of brilliant yellow dandelions.* The small flowers of the chamomile, like tiny daisies, were so easily disguised amidst the brilliant yellow of the dandelions that they could be easily confused to an unaware eye as just another weed. But both plants were essential, and they needed to be protected and properly utilized, rather than dismissed as weeds and discarded.

I kept a gathering basket handy by the water pump and used it to collect my clippings. Poor Nina, so human. I would have known this salve like the back of my hand if I needed it, but being fae and glamoured, the aging process was, well, weird. Thankfully, I had my "cook" books for the likes of our darling girl.

I followed the distinct instructions in the HOHUM, which really weren't so distinct, a pinch of this here and shred of that there, a squirt of the dandelion milk, simmer for however long, and voila! A salve. This was one cookbook that relied on the cook to know what to do.

At four o'clock sharp, there was a knock at the front door. My skin salve for the seamstress had just finished curing.

"Come in! It's open!" I hollered at the foyer, assuming they could hear my teeny weeny voice. But of course, it was Mat, and he had the keen hearing of an owl, so the door creaked on its hinges as he opened it and led his beloved Nina in before him, ducking his head very low to maneuver the threshold.

What wasn't included in the recipe for the ointment was faerie dust, but I added a pinch of it to speed up its progress.

Nina was in a black cashmere sweater with pearl buttons up to the neck. She daintily unfastened the exquisite buttons to reveal the imprint imbedded on her sternum directly above her breast.

"Are you sure you want this to disappear, Nina? This mixture will do that. No matter what happens to the necklace, you can always have this," I warned her in advance of applying the aid.

She and Mat glanced at one another, with that special knowing look between true loves.

Mat responded on her nod, "You are probably right, Aunt Siobhan."

"No worries, this keeps for a long time. If you change your mind, let me know. If you don't, someone else will probably desire it! It may even contain a little something special for your later years." I winked at Mat.

We enjoyed a bit of tea together. Well, Nina was having espresso, but no matter. After a while, I had to rush them on their way. I knew they thought they were accommodating "the old lady," but really, I had things to do!

Wu only had four days. I assumed the first day started tomorrow, but I should double check with Barbie. Nevertheless, that didn't give anyone much time. It was now close to dusk, and Wu must already be registered with the Court and returned to his quarters at the inn.

I had no way of getting in touch with him, and even though I didn't want him to get the impression that I was anxious to see him, I didn't want to waste a spare second figuring out what needed to be done so that he could accomplish his mission.

Wait! I do have a way! I'll call Michaela at the inn. He either has a house phone or she can relay a message to him.

"Michaela? This is Teeny Weeny," I responded to the answer on the other end of the phone, pronouncing her name "Mi-hae-la" like her aunt Luisa, her "mammie" did.

She confirmed that there indeed was a house phone in Wu's cabin, and that she would connect me.

I took a big gulp, not really knowing what I was going to say, but hoping it would come to me when I heard his voice.

"Hello?" And there it was, that tingly feeling in my fingertips, toes, earlobes, and nose.

"Dr. Wu, it's Madame Tahini. I was thinking, well, uh . . . maybe we should get started examining the amulet right away. I mean so we don't waste any time, since the Court limited you to four days. Oh, and by the way, how did the tattoo go?" I added the last bit so he didn't think that I was so anxious to see him or anything.

"I agree with you completely. I'm obviously not going anywhere, since I am under house arrest, so you can come by whenever you would like. The tattooing went well. Miss Adelaide Beaumont is quite the talent. I now have a tattoo of a crane. It is beyond me how she knew that is my spirit guide."

"Yes, Addie has a special gift for that sort of thing. I can be there in about an hour. Goodbye." I clicked off and went about preparing for my meeting with Tang Wu.

CHAPTER 14

TEENY WEENY

*W*hen I arrived, there was a nice little fire blazing in the small hearth in the living area of his cottage. He took my coat and offered me some tea. Naturally, I accepted. The green tea was really quite good.

I had the amulet with me, but as it was damaged, it really was not going to be of much use to us, so we were stuck with trying to manipulate the small picture on my phone.

"Maybe I should ask Michaela if she could print this out?" I suggested.

We were sitting side by side on the settee in front of the fireplace, and it was nearly unnerving the vibrations I felt and that creamy buttery taste on my lips when his hand met mine holding the cell phone.

"We may need to do that, but for now, let me get a notepad and jot down what we can see in this photo."

He got up and left for a brief moment, returning with a hotel-style pad and a pen both inscribed with the words "Whisper Falls Inn" with a simple but stunning logo. He sat right back down next to me and began to write the characters that appeared in the flipped photo version of Nina's embedded scar.

"Siobhan . . . oh, I'm sorry, may I call you Siobhan?" he began, and then stopped himself.

He says my name so delicately, pronouncing it more like chiffon, that I can almost taste a creamy chiffon pie with extra whipped cream on top. It makes me downright woozy when he says my name that way.

"Oh yes, please do! I'm not sure how I should address you, though, given you have more than one name?" *Look who's talking.*

"My given name is Qiángdà. It means powerful. The dialect is a bit difficult to maneuver, so Tang Da or Tang for short is fine. As to the amulet, typically these spells begin at the north edge of the amulet. The yin-yang is the guide for the north and south. Yin is north and yang is south."

He was actually writing down the ideograms as they appeared in the photo, keeping them in their circular motif. I watched, mesmerized and silent, as he made quarter turns with the photo using his fingers and then manually turned the Whisper Falls Inn notepad in the same quarterly fashion. He made a rough sketch of the yin-yang in the center of this circle of figures.

When he completed the entire circular chart of characters, an almost blank stare overcame his demeanor. I could practically see a giant question mark above his head as he quizzically pondered the symbols he had scripted.

"What is it?" I finally broke the silence, and the trance to which he had succumbed.

"It appears this is not so much a spell to break a curse as it is a recipe."

I'm good with that! I can do recipes, even when my cookbook doesn't really give great direction.

"What does that mean?" I was trying to be patient, but between tingling and creamery butter, I wasn't sure if I could hold out much longer. I needed a rest!

"It is talking about the *Dan* of *Běnzhí*. It is the Elixir of Essence. I have heard about it, but as far as I know, no one actually knows how to make it. This apparently is the recipe."

"What does that mean?" I was starting to sound like a broken record.

"Essence is everything about a person, more than just their soul. It is their life, blood, innate characteristics, their spirit, their beliefs, and even their destiny. The Elixir of Essence can only be used when one's essence is taken from them unnaturally. Some of this makes sense, but some I am not sure what it means. Like here." He pointed to a grouping of swashes and slashes. "Translated it says Hair of Crane. But cranes do not have hair. If it meant feather or down, it would have said that, but this is specific as to hair. It bewilders me. Then there is this . . ." He pointed at another set of hieroglyphs that made no sense to me, so I was just intrigued that he even knew what it represented. "This says the light of *Xiānnǚ*. I really don't know what that means at all. I mean, I know *Xiānnǚ*, but I am not sure what the 'light of' is really referring to."

He said this word *Xiānnǚ* something like tschen gnu (like the wildebeest) but it was so foreign to me, I had no idea.

"What does that mean? That word, tschen gnu?" Okay, I kicked it up a notch so as not to sound like a total broken record.

"Ahh, well, interestingly enough, it means fairy or sprite. Like you, I'm guessing." And he said this with a jesting spirit and a twinkle in his eye that sent me reeling.

That was my opportunity to bid him goodnight before I did something really dangerous, like kiss him. "Then I think we should both sleep on those words tonight. Maybe the Spirit Crane will enlighten you, or my fae spirits will send me a message."

He stood up and offered me his helping hand in a gentlemanly gesture. I did take it, cringing inside all the time, knowing what his touch did to me, and now not only creamy butter but sweet honey was piercing my tongue. *What a mess I am!*

Now that he had his little map of the pendant, I took my phone and placed it in my skirt pocket, as he got my coat and assisted me in donning it. We both agreed that I would contact him in the morning, after breakfast, and I exited as quickly as possible.

CHAPTER 15

WU

I hoped I had not offended her. She left in such a hurry that I feared she did not wish to be near me. She always seemed to have the strangest reaction when I so much as touched her hand. But her hand was so soft, so small, so wonderful, I couldn't help myself.

She was small, but she was so powerful. She was *Qiángdà Xiānnǚ*, a powerful fae! But she had a power over me that again I could not explain. I'd never felt this way with anyone, let alone a teeny weeny woman.

I needed to concentrate on this Elixir of Essence. I would only have one chance to get it right. Like this evening might have been my chance to get it right with Siobhan, but I was sure I botched that one.

Really, you HAVE to concentrate!

I looked at my drawing of the amulet on the pad I had jotted on. It began from the north of the ornament, "The *Dan* of *Běnzhí* only when *Běnzhí* is stolen. Dram of Dragon's Water, one Hair of Crane, light of *Xiānnǚ*."

Really the only thing I understood was the Dram of Dragon's Water. That was the water from Tiger Pond. It was believed that the Dragon drank from the pond; that was why it was used when making Dragon's Well tea. It was the same pond that the great Spirit Crane drank from, but I could guarantee she had never left a hair behind, even as an apparition. So even if it was speaking of her appearance in human form, how could I have obtained a hair from an apparition anyway? And then . . . there was the light of fae.

Ah, Siobhan, you are my light, but I am not sure how that is going to translate into an elixir.

Stop it, man! Concentrate!

Really, it was no use. I could only think of her this evening. Her big eyes, far too large for her face, with those long dark lashes. Her little pursed lips, always puckered like she was tasting something she was unfamiliar with. The way she constantly wiggled her fingers and her toes. Oh my, it might just have driven me to insanity, but if nothing else, it had all worked up an appetite.

I guessed I was stuck with ordering room service or delivery. I heard the teens in town talking about the taco truck. It sounded interesting enough, maybe not so different from a good mu shu pork. They kind of acted like it was a new invention, this food truck thing. Centuries ago, we always had at least one or two carts in the town square. How else was a young man to survive if there were not purveyors of pot stickers and pork buns?

I picked up the house phone and dialed the front desk. The lovely voice of Miss Michaela came from the other end of the wire.

I asked her about the food truck, and she informed me that Tacos for Daze was run by Sky Spill Water. *Sounds like a combination of Hollywood and Navajo . . . I like his name.* I could hear her rustling through papers, then she started reeling off the short menu. I picked out a pulled pork something or other, then thanked the young woman for her assistance and hung up.

A little food, a little sleep, then maybe I would be able to concentrate on the Elixir of Essence and my mission.

~

TEENY WEENY

Why was it I always seemed to be running away from Tim Wu, or Tang Da, or well, *him*? I really only wanted to stay, but it felt, sounded, tasted, and smelled so awkward to me. He was even upsetting my already screwed-up sensory system. I just never seemed to be able to think clearly when I was near him.

Well, I was home and safe in my little place. I grabbed my fleece nightgown, wrapped myself in my robe, curled up with a good book (*Ancient Arts and Mystics*, naturally), and settled my body into my comfy down mattress to rest this weary head of mine.

I fell asleep somewhere on page 322 or thereabouts (the number may or may not be of importance, one never really knew for sure) of my encyclopedia. I was reading about the *Xiānnǚ*, the fairies of the Orient, when I nodded off.

The crane in my dream from the other night returned again, but this time as a woman. She stood next to Wu, in his natural state, with his white hair and long beard. Actually it wasn't so much that she was standing beside him. It was more like she was in him, around him, and through him.

The next vision of the night was of my own Goddess Brid. My guide, she was the fire of hearth, forge, and inspiration. It was through her and her fellow gods and goddesses that I existed still today. She appeared in her ethereal form, carrying a flame upon her open hand and an olive branch in the other. She was adorned in a tapestry that depicted the essence of spring.

Light of *Xiānnǚ*—was this it? The flame that Brid held in her palm? She and her flame were my guide, but I did not believe that was something that could be captured and used. Certainly not in a country thousands of miles from here and certainly not in a time hundreds and hundreds of years ago.

That was the last vision of the night. After that, I slept as if I hadn't slept for a week, which certainly felt like it was the case. I awoke well after the dawn's light broke through my curtains. I felt like the sunlight pouring into the bedroom was all the enlightening I need. I found myself heaving a calm sigh, as if a heavy weight had just been lifted from my chest. That was, until I heard the clamoring of four pixies in my kitchen. Did I leave the door unlocked? They were pixies, so they certainly could manage the little crack under the door that never quite was flush with the doorstep. They had never done that before, so I was guessing it was due to my own absentmindedness from this entire calamity.

I hurried downstairs and found Tierri and Aeiri over the sink, trying to work the latch on the window above it to allow Cyllene in, who was not so patiently waiting to enter. This was well past my normal wake-up time; in fact it was eight o'clock. *Eight o'clock? Oh geez, what the heck happened?*

Enya and Ushka were trying to figure out how to brew my morning tea, and it even looked like they had it covered. *There is hope!* The good news, I guess, was that I had been so busy between Wu, the Court, Nina and Mat, and of course, the amulet, that Cyllene's megaphone was still in the exact place we left it yesterday morning. So really, all I needed to do was sit down at the table and let everyone take their places. That equated to the pixies going into the parlor to presumably wrestle one another, and Cyllene alighting by the funnel.

"Well? What's going on? You are out late! You slept in late! You have a funny look on your face!" Cyllene's admonishments and questions came barreling through the funnel.

"Silly Annie, everything is fine!" I said to her, but I didn't completely believe it myself, especially the "funny look" comment.

"Cyllene! See-lee-nee! And it's clear everything is not 'fine.' What happened at Court? Where were you last night? Why aren't you up at dawn like normal?"

Sheesh, she is now sounding like she's my nanny and not the pixies'. Wait . . . What? Weren't the pixies letting Cyllene in and making my tea too? Maybe I am the one who needs a nanny.

I apologized for my behavior and continued to tell her about the whole proceeding in Court, the ruling they made on Wu's term here in Havenwood Falls, the salve for Nina, the meeting with Tang Da . . .

"Tang what?" Cyllene stopped me at that point. So now I had to fill her in about how Tang Da Wu was posing as Dr. Timothy Wu and why.

I would tell you she lifted one of her eyebrows suspiciously, if she had eyebrows, but her complexion was so multicolored she looked like an illustrated lady. There was a colorful menagerie of hues above her vibrant eyes that gave the same impression as raising an eyebrow.

After explaining the task that Wu and I had been assigned by the Court, I told her about the visions I had last night.

"So you said Addie gave him a tattoo of a crane? And he said that's his spirit guide?"

I nodded in response while sipping a pretty well-brewed cup of tea.

"Then I think that part of the visions I understand. The crane actually represents your Dr. Wu, or I guess the real Wu. He and his spirit guide are meshed. His hair is the Hair of the Crane," Cyllene stated rather matter-of-factly.

"Silly Annie! I mean, Cyllene, you are brilliant!"

"One doesn't live some eight hundred-odd years being a soul of a tree without learning a thing or two along the way," she said proudly, and for a moment, her mosaic skin took on all its former radiancy.

"Well, this I have to share with Tang! Hopefully, he has determined the other piece of the puzzle."

"On a first name basis, I see." She harrumphed. "Explains your funny look."

I guess she was right about learning a thing or two over the course of a few centuries, because she might have nailed this one too.

I ran upstairs to change clothes and just as I reached the top landing, I heard my cell phone buzzing on the end table. I ran to the phone expecting to see Barbie's name, or even Mat's, but the caller ID revealed "Whisper Falls Inn."

"Hello?" I answered the call.

Michaela was on the other end, and she said that Dr. Wu was calling, and wanted to know if she should transfer his call. I of course said yes, and she connected us, or whatever it was—merged the call, swapped the call—it was all new to me.

"Siobhan?" the inquiring voice came through after a clicking sound.

"Tang, good morning! Sorry, I'm running a bit late."

"I took the liberty of having some blueberry scones delivered from Coffee Haven. I hope that's okay."

"Perfect, they are the best! I should be there in about fifteen minutes." Then I added, "I received a little inspiration this morning that might help us move this mysterious mixture along. See you soon!" I hung up quickly, since I was practically drooling with a taste of the butter and honey on my lips just from hearing his voice, let alone the thought of Coffee Haven scones for breakfast.

As I entered the cottage, the smell of freshly baked blueberry scones was wafting in the air, and Tang was busily nibbling away at one of them.

"These are incredible! I've never tasted anything so divine!" he said waving a half-eaten scone in the air while motioning me in.

"Of course they are. They have a touch of magic." I smiled, knowing these were far better than my faerie cakes.

"Speaking of which . . ." He paused, finishing the biscuit in his hand. "I believe I have determined the part of the spell regarding the Light of *Xiānnǚ*. This morning I remembered our little fight—again I humbly apologize for that . . ."

I waved my hand as if it were nothing. "Forgiven, forgotten . . . forge on!"

"The wand that you wield, it has a tip that glows like a nebula. I think that is it—the light of the fae, a fairy's wand. There's only one problem . . ." He hesitated.

"Yes?"

"You are the only fae I know. Back home, in my time, it is not a realm I associate with. When I return, there will not be enough time for me to find a *Xiānnǚ* to help, assuming one would be willing. I think I am going to need you to come with me. That is, if we can figure out the other meaning of the amulet's message."

I was taken aback by his suggestion that I go to China with him, and not only China, but a China way before I was even born. I would deal with that idea later, if it were something that could even be accomplished. First I wanted to share with him what Cyllene had discerned.

"Ah, the Hair of the Crane! I think you are correct. It is not a feather, but neither is it a crane. You are the crane!" I told him excitedly.

"Me? Why me?" he bewildered.

"You live in the divination of the Spirit Crane. She is your guide, as Brid, the goddess of spring, is mine. She is a part of you. In you and around you always. You are her manifestation in this earthly realm. It is *your* hair that is required."

Then the light dawned in his eyes. He stood up quickly, spreading scone crumbs all over the floor. *The pixies would have a feast with those.* He hurried over to the table where he had left the notepad with his rudimentary drawings, and re-read the scripture.

"I see it now! It is more detailed than just hair of crane. It says specifically 'the white hair of a crane's neck.' I was focusing on the wrong thing. That would be a hair from my beard. Well, the beard I will have when I return home," he said as he stroked the finely trimmed dark goatee of Timothy Wu. "The other part makes more sense about it being your wand, now that I am reading the details. It says a 'touch of the Light of *Xiānnǚ*.' Spirit Crane told me that I will need what I learn here to accomplish my journey in the past. You, dear Siobhan, you are my teacher! I definitely need you!"

"Say I would go with you, how do you propose that be accomplished? You told the Court you were able to enter this time because Dr. Wu was your descendant. I am quite sure I have no Chinese ancestry in my blood." He raised an eyebrow, and I stopped him before he could even say another word. "No! I'm not taking a DNA test!"

"Then I fear I am right back where I started, failing." He turned away, but not without me seeing the forlorn look on his face. He uttered as he returned the notepad to the table, "If only you had some fae magic that could move you to another place."

"Well, I can ripple," I responded, "but I don't know about in time. I've only rippled in space."

He turned about again to face me, his eyes bright once more.

"Time and space—they are relative. One cannot be without the other. Tell me about it."

So I explained to him about the ripple. How I could go from one place to another in a matter of minutes, or less, sometimes more. I got into the stipple in the ripple, that little wrinkle that does not guarantee that I will arrive in the new space without losing or gaining time, sometimes minutes, days, even weeks. If I could use the ripple to move in time, it may have a similar (or opposite, depending on how you looked at it) effect on the space. Maybe I could get to the right time, but perhaps I'd be in Timbuktu instead of Tiger Pond, or whatever the place was he said he was from.

He massaged his chin again, then said, "I know the exact time I will return. It will be nine p.m., 13th of October 3519."

"3519? It's only 2019 now. I thought you were going back in time!" I heard myself screeching this.

"So sorry, that is the Chinese calendar year. For Westerners, it would be 800 CE. You will be able to find Tiger Pond by letting the crane constellation guide you, as it will point you directly to its location."

"I don't know that I have ever heard of the crane constellation. I will have to review my charts."

"I believe you may find it by the name Grus. In fact, the only star that will be visible then will be the Alpha Grus, or Alnair."

"I see, so you want me to go back more than one thousand years, then find you by a constellation that I may only be able to identify by a single star. That's what you're saying, right?"

"Uh, correct," was all he could say.

"Well, that's a lot to take in, and a good deal more to think about. We still have a few days, and if I do agree to go, and I'm not saying I do, I have plenty of studying to do first." With that, I grabbed a scone and left.

CHAPTER 16

TEENY WEENY

I spent the rest of the day and night reading everything I could find about time travel and reviewing my own sky charts. I did find the crane constellation he spoke of, but even if I did go, I had to familiarize myself not only with it but also its location on that day and time.

I had arranged with Barbie to meet her at the Broastful Brew the next morning, and this time I was more than prompt. I sat at the table waiting for her for a change.

I wasted no time. As soon as she sat down, I filled her in on the amulet, the spell—rather the recipe—and what Wu and I had come up with. Naturally, that included his grandiose scheme of my traveling in time to meet up with him in some land far far away, like a faerie tale that even I had a hard time swallowing.

She took a sip of coffee, then leaned back in her chair. After a minute or so of contemplating my words, she said, "Seems like the two of you are moving right along. What do you think about this time travel thing? Is that something you can do? Is it something you want to do?"

"Well, if saving the poor child is truly essential to our very existence, then yes, it is something I want to do. Is it something I can do? I'm not really sure. It's a little frightening." *Actually, it's a lot frightening.* "I'm assuming I can get there and back again. I've been thinking about whether the ripple would work with time, but I've never done that, so I just don't know."

"You do have a couple of days left. You might want to start practicing. Meanwhile, I'll talk with some of the Court members, maybe even Dr. Sam Fraser, the new professor at Halvard Campus—he teaches interdimensional exploration and time travel and has some experience himself. He might be able to provide a portal, or something of the sort, just in case." I wasn't sure if she was mimicking my *just in case* to tease me, or if she really meant a portal just in case.

The Luna Coven did a time travel spell for Joe Greg, a young wolf shifter, over the summer, but that was only a few years backward and nowhere near the distance. They only sent him to Houston for the year 2012. Even that was a big risk for the Luna Coven.

After our meeting, I just kept repeating on my way home, "Practice, portal, portal, practice." The portal idea was intriguing, and for some reason I felt it was safer, mainly because it would be here in Havenwood Falls, where I belonged, when I belonged! But that was a "just in case," like Barbie said, so the practice part had to come first, and I had to get started right away.

I decided to try it out with just a few months ago, when I broke the curse on my brother Grenfold and reunited him with the mermaid Coralie at Peacock Lake. When I got home, I went straight into the salon, wasting no time. I closed my eyes and concentrated on the image of that moment with Gruff by my side, ready to break the curse. The ripple began, the atmosphere around me started to waver, and as it did, so did I, melting into that wave. In an instant I was at the edge of the lake, looking at Gruff's forlorn face and the red-haired beauty poking her head out from the turquoise and teal waters.

It worked! I can do it!

I was about to say the words that broke the curse when I realized I did not have my wand with me. *Oh dear goddesses, what have I done? Did I mess this whole moment up by rippling without being prepared?* I panicked and immediately reversed my concentration back to the salon and the moment I got home from the Brew.

The ripple returned me to my home once again. Without wasting a second, I ran to my bedroom and the bedside table where my wand was stored in the keyless safe. After passing my hand over the pearlescent latch to pop it open, I grabbed my wand from its velvet bed. I closed my eyes once again and placed the scene at Peacock Lake from last May into my mind's eye, praying that it was still there.

The air around me vacillated as I slipped into the ripple and appeared at the precipice of Peacock Lake, with everyone in place as before. *Whew! That was close!*

I touched the glowing tip of my wand to Gruff's head and said the magic words that broke the curse. I witnessed once again the serene transformation of Gruff into my beautiful brother Grenfold, who then kissed me on the forehead and said, "Thank you! Make amends with Father! I'll love you always, sister!" With that, he joined the lovely sea maiden in Peacock Lake and swam away.

I was so relieved that I had done no damage to their destiny. This time-space continuum was going to be tricky. I also realized that I'd better take my wand with me when I tried this again, just in case.

Home again in the right time, well, the present time anyway, I decided to relax and have some tea. I also found myself starving, so a snack or a grab-it was in order. But with such little time left before Wu must depart, I would have to practice the time ripple again, but farther away and further back in time. A few months and nearby did not seem to be a real challenge. Hopefully, it would be the same with a more difficult journey.

Later in the evening, I reminisced about Grenfold and Coralie, and how in love they were and how patient that love was to remain so strong after hundreds of years apart from one another. I decided to try to return to the moment when Father, the great King Ian of the spring fae, was about to curse my brother. This time I would stand up to him and stop him. I realized that now! Maybe I could save the two lovers eons of heartache, and maybe my mother, Queen Rose, in the process.

I stood by the wardrobe in my bedroom, holding my wand in both hands, not about to take the chance of losing it in some tidal wave of time and space, and focused on the Isle of Gwynf'l and the emerald fields of shamrocks that flocked the hillside. I imagined the moment my father began his chant more than 550 years ago, the one I dreamed about every year on the spring equinox. The space around me undulated, and I was gently pulled into it.

This time, however, when I appeared on the other side of the ripple, I was not on the hillside with my father, mother, and Grenfold. Instead, I found myself in our home, a quaint thatched hut, which was quite a distance from that field. The surroundings were familiar—a kettle of soup simmered in the hearth and my mother's strings of flowers she made each morning for our necklaces and bracelets were aligned on the table. At least this told me that the time was somewhat close, and I was on the right island, if not the exact place I had intended to be.

So there was a stipple in a time ripple too. I figured I'd better explore the area and determine how far off in time I might truly be. Last time I traveled from here in a ripple, I had lost weeks! As I exited the cabin, I grabbed one of the daisy chains and placed it around my neck. I couldn't help myself. I had forgotten all about them.

I headed toward the hill where the incident occurred, and right before I got out of the wooded section where our home was lodged, I heard my father already halfway through his curse. I ran as fast as I could, but I could not reach them in time to stop him. I came to an abrupt halt as I saw and heard my poor brother Grenfold turn into a misshapen soul and scamper away as my father ordered him to crawl under a rock.

The agony and grief I felt that day came back to me, as it did every time the dream recurred. Unlike the first time, when I turned away from my father and went after Grenfold, now poor Gruff, I was watching my father from this distance. Father had fallen to his knees and began to weep.

"What have I done? Oh dear lords, what have I done? This power is not for me!" I heard him crying into his hands. Then I saw him thrashing at the dirt, digging up the soil with his bare hands. He placed his wand in the hole he had created, stood up, and kicked the dirt back onto it, then rolled a large rock over the top.

I guess it was not meant to be for me to save Grenfold and Coralie from their estrangement. Perhaps this was necessary for them to be together in Havenwood Falls. I ran to my father and hugged him, telling him it would be okay, and Grenfold and I would always love him. My mother was grabbing her stomach in pain, and tears flowed from her beautiful azure eyes. I heard my father telling her if the pain was still that bad, they should go see the witch for another dose of brew. I had no idea my mother was ill. I thought she died from the heartache of her only son being cursed to live as a troll.

My father wrapped his arm around my mother and gently led her back home. After they abandoned this fae-forsaken site, I sat on the rock and cried an eternity of tears for all I had misunderstood. As I lifted my hand to wipe my tears, wishing I were in my own room with a good down pillow to soak up this mess, I accidentally touched my wand to my the tip of my nose.

There came an enormous boom, like the sound of a volcanic eruption. The air puckered and ruffled, but not anything like a ripple. A bolt of bright purple lightning flashed down from the clear blue sky and hit the ground next to the spot that Father had buried his wand.

There was now a large glowing amaranthine colored hole, but not in the ground. It was standing right before me, in midair, like a doorway to a deep dark tunnel. *Is this a portal?*

I took a chance and walked through the threshold. I felt my body swirl through an amethyst sea of time and space, all glowing with sparks of yellow, blue, and green. Bolts of white lightning flashed before me and beside me.

I heard a tremendous rumble and another explosion, then suddenly I was blasted through another hole, and found myself standing beside the wardrobe in my very own bedroom in Havenwood Falls. *It was a portal!*

CHAPTER 17

WU

*a*s uncomfortable as it was to be under house arrest, I was delighted that Siobhan was working with me on this project. When she was in my company, nothing else seemed to matter. I had full confidence that she was a strong fae. How else could she have such power over me and my affections? She called early this morning to let me know that she could indeed ripple in time and space simultaneously. I had no doubt, but the diminutive dear did not have enough faith in herself.

She said she had a few questions for me, so that she could prepare for the journey, though she hadn't quite yet decided if she was going. I guessed that wasn't true. Otherwise why would she be experimenting with her ripple?

I heard a tiny rap on the door, and I knew it was her sweet little hand knocking upon the wood.

"Come in; it's open!" I responded to the sound.

There she was, all four foot five of her. I noticed her hair looked different. It seemed like there was glitter in it or something. I asked her about it.

She stroked her hair, and I watched as it seemed to glow with a glistening white undertone, the colorful sparkles moving about.

"Oh, this? Well, apparently the time-space travel has some unusual effects. I doubt there is a hairdresser who could quite accomplish this technique."

I found it enchanting, as I did her.

"On to business," she interrupted my musings. "So, first, I'd like to know what happens to Dr. Timothy Wu when you return?"

"Currently, Dr. Wu is in a fugue state, in his own home. When I return, he will awake from that state, without any memory of the last week or so. No harm will have come to him other than the loss of a few days. He will feel extremely rested and recharged, as if he had been on the best vacation ever."

"Well, I'm happy to hear that, and I suspect the teenagers in town, who are all infatuated with him, will be too. Next, I'm going to need an image of the place that I'll be able to fix in my mind's eye. I don't even think a photograph will work. So I'm not sure how we will overcome that obstacle."

"Let me get my compass. That might do the trick," I replied as I headed to the closet for my black bag.

"Uh, Tang, if a photograph won't do it, I doubt a compass will."

"I said *my* compass." I returned to my favorite fae. Now I was glad that I never had any dealings with a *Xiānnǚ* before, as I doubted I would ever have been able to concentrate on my profession.

I held the round gold box before her, which looked everything like a pocket watch or navigator's compass, until I pushed the little button that popped open the lid. Instead of finding a minute and second hand, or the twelve points of the compass and a magnetic needle to gauge the direction, the inside revealed something similar to a mirror, but not exactly. The image of Tiger Pond, the temple, the plum and cherry blossom trees, and a myriad of birds including cranes came into view. But this was a living image, the water shimmering, hummingbirds twittering around the cherry blossoms as their petals flowed to and fro in the wind, and bright gold-and-white koi jumping in and out of the water.

"This is how I will find my way home." I placed my finger on the glass, and the image changed to the Wudang Mountains, lush with greenery, the mists from the multitude of secluded waterfalls rising and working their way like a fog throughout the upper edges of the dense forest. A falcon was flying high above the treetops. Again with my finger I traced the cover, and the image turned into one of my small village, with children playing near the community well, and carts of fruits and vegetables lining the dirt paths.

"This is amazing! I think I can work with these moving pictures. It feels like I am really there," she responded, while doing that little jig of hers I found so charming. I guessed this meant she was really going.

"You can take this for tonight to familiarize yourself with the area and get a fix in your mind of where you are going." I handed her the imaging contraption.

"Yes, thank you! I will study it the rest of the day and evening, then we should be able to report to the Court that we have figured out how to accomplish our mission. I mean, your mission."

She's going! Thank you, Great Spirit Crane, for your blessings!

CHAPTER 18

TEENY WEENY

I spent the entire rest of the day mesmerized with the impressions that wafted in and out of the circular frame of the compass. *I think I'm going to call this the Come Home Compass.*

It was a truly amazing little gadget. I even saw the poor young boy on his luxurious throne-style bed, on the brink of death. A lot of good all that luxury did for him now. It looked like a white-haired shaman and a teeny weeny woman were what he was going to need most. I saw the emperor and empress fretting over the sickly child, and another woman—at least, I thought it was a woman—in a simple flat black jacket, with a long braid trailing down to her waist from the nape of her neck. She was not much taller than I, maybe an inch or two.

I texted Barbie right before I went to bed to let her know that we were ready to report to the court.

BS: Great! And you?
TW: Yes, I'm going w/
BS: Woohoo! LOL WuHoo!
Sheesh! I'm not sure this texting is a good thing. WuHoo? From Barbie?

I met up with Tang Da Wu at his cottage the next morning. Sheriff Kasun was already on the porch, waiting for my arrival. He would escort us to the Court. After all, Wu was technically still under arrest.

We kept it pretty short and simple, explaining how we were able to use the reversed photo, and how between the two of us, we figured out the elements for Dr. Wu to return to his appointed time and place and perform the cure. I acknowledged to the Court that I was aware my part of this journey had a few wrinkles, a.k.a. stipples, but regardless, I should be able to return in a day or two—well, a week tops. *I hope!* So I should be safe within the memory ward boundaries.

We also recited how the real Dr. Wu would reawaken once Tang had returned. Maybe the Court would still want to offer him the invite, as he sounded like a good fit with Sun & Moon Academy and its students.

We received the blessing from the Court to proceed. Barbie and Ric were to oversee Wu's departure (to ensure he actually did depart). I was to take care of my individual "travel" plans, as I saw fit.

As we exited the Court, I returned Tang's compass to him and asked him about the other woman in moving picture.

"Oh, that is Mai Li. She is my Mickey Mouse."

Ah, I was right. It is a woman! "Your Mickey Mouse?"

"When the two English marms weren't chattering away, I had the privilege of watching Walt Disney's *Fantasia* on the airplane. Mai Li is my sorcerer's apprentice. She has been assisting me and learning the arts of the Wu for many years. She is almost ready for her mastery."

We agreed that I was to meet him in the prince's chambers, as close as possible to nine o'clock in the evening. He showed me on the sky chart where that one stupid star was supposed to be in the sky at that time. *Yikes!*

I prepared myself as best as I was able. Cyllene was literally hovering over me as I skittered around, trying to decide what I needed. She buzzed incessantly above my head, trying to tell me something.

We went into the kitchen, where the funnel ensemble was still in place. *Dang, this has been a busy week!*

She set herself up to her megaphonic instrument. "Siobhan, you are going to a place and time you have never been. You are not taking a trip on a bus! Trust me on this—you need yourself and your wand.

That's it! The rest is up to you and your magic. By the way, I like your hair."

She's right, of course. Gotta hand it to a dryad of eight hundred years, give or take a score or two.

I left Cyllene in charge of the pixies, which she was extremely delighted about. Why did it take me so long to figure that one out?

My cell phone vibrated, and there was another text from Barbie.

BS: Done! WuBeGone!

Okay, that's really weird, because she wasn't there, and I was pretty sure I didn't tell her that part. I will have to think about that later. This meant it was my turn.

TW: K! C ya! Sooner/Later/Whatever

It really was my turn.

I went to my bedroom and looked at the new radiating portal next to the wardrobe—well, almost embedded in it. *Can I use this to get back from China's Zhou Dynasty?* I took a chance again and entered the portal.

I found myself swirling through the complexity of purplish-red gases and prismatic sparks and bolts, only to find myself back on the hillside of the Isle of Gwynf'l. *Well, that won't work.* Apparently this was a doorway between then and now, and here and there.

So much for my entryway to above and beyond. Seemed I was stuck with the ripple and my wand.

I made sure I had my wand held tightly in both hands. I focused on the living image of the young boy on his death bed in a land far away, in a time far behind, as it appeared in Wu's Come Home Compass. I also concentrated on the sky chart path with that crazy Alnair that was supposed to be my guiding star.

Oh my gosh! I'm here! At least, I think I'm here. Well, I wasn't exactly in the emperor's mansion, nor at Tiger Pond or the temple. I found myself standing under a waterfall, getting drenched. But it was definitely not the Great Havenwood Falls, and it was not the three sister falls at Peacock Lake. I looked around, and the area was thick with tall, fibrous bamboo, and I even saw a panda bear munching on a stem! Heavy dark green vines looped from each and every tree in this lush forestry.

I made it to China! Not where I was supposed to be—there was a stipple. *That's one!* I hoped the timing was at least close. Now I had to see if I could even find the bright crane star Wu told me to follow. If it wasn't even visible, I definitely had the wrong time. Really? What was I thinking?

~

WU

I am home again! Thanks again to you, Great Spirit Crane.

There was a peace and serenity in that knowledge. So why was I feeling nervous and apprehensive? I had no idea when Siobhan, my teeny weeny fae, my *Xiànnǚ*, was going to show up. Or where she would show up, even if she did. Without her, I could not cure the boy. However, I had no choice but to leave; the Court made sure of that.

Without her, I felt lost! This emotion was on a completely different plane than I had ever experienced. If she arrived, we could cure the prince, we could save the dynasty, and as long as my people were diligent, we could save the faith.

I wanted to be with her always. This would be the end for me as a shaman. I had served my rulers well.

"Master Wu!" my apprentice, Mai Li addressed me. "Where have you been?"

"On my mission, Mai Li! I have found the cure, and we must get everything ready. The boy has not a minute to lose. I need you to fill this beaker with water from Tiger Pond, then meet me in the child's chambers forthwith. There is a *Xiànnǚ* that is required. I am waiting for her arrival."

"*Her?* A *Xiànnǚ*? What is this? You have nothing to do with *Xiànnǚ*."

"It is not your concern, Mai Li! She is necessary to heal the prince and let him have his destiny!"

"Very well, Master Wu. I will get the water and bring it to the palace." She bowed to me in acquiescence, or so I thought.

Sometimes that woman could be so difficult! No wonder I never married!

TEENY WEENY

I had no idea when I was. I definitely knew I was in the right place, well, country at least. I didn't have a clue if I was anywhere near the right century, let alone the right day and time.

Everything I read told me that this crane star, the Alnair in the Grus constellation, was rarely visible in China. *Yet Tang Wu insisted it could guide me? I am crazy!*

Perhaps he was right. The day and time I was supposed to be here was the day and time you could actually see that star. I started thinking about Mat, my nephew, and his joyous compilation of fae and owl. How he could see and hear things, even in the dark, that no other could see or hear. How he could soar through the Havenwood Falls night skies without fear or worry, the moon reflecting on his perfectly white wings, able to navigate all of it by the stars and his pure love.

With all of those thoughts in my mind, and not even realizing it, I stepped into the ripple.

I found myself no longer in the waterfalls somewhere in the Wudang Mountains—*I guess that's where I was*—but actually on the edge of Tiger Pond. Better yet! That crane star thing was not only reflecting off the pond, it was magnified! It was magnificent!

WU

I arranged all of the necessary items to cure the boy in accordance with the spell divulged on the amulet. The temple held not only my equipment, but my secrets as well.

I sent Mai Li to retrieve the Dragon Water from Tiger Pond. I looked up at the sky and saw the Great Crane's beak shining brightly through the misty night sky. It was time. I was here when I was supposed to be here. I hoped my love—I mean, my little fae—would also arrive on time.

This had always been a little iffy.

There was a strange waver in the air, and Tiger Pond emitted an ambiance that was almost like a mirage effect. There she was! She had just rippled to the edge of the lake! The cranes drinking from the water took flight upon her arrival in this unusual appearance.

The next thing I saw was Mai Li running toward her. I assumed that she was greeting her, as Mai Li knew we needed her to ensure our destiny.

Oh, Great Crane! Mai Li just pushed Siobhan, my love, into Tiger Pond! Blasphemy!

～

TEENY WEENY

This pond was astounding! It almost seemed like diamonds were floating and glistening in the lake. I thought I could love this place. In so many ways, it reminded me of the Isle of the Gwynf'l, but far more lush and brilliant. I saw my own reflection in this sylvan pond. It revealed that I was now cloaked in a white robe, my hair totally white, except there was a rainbow effect, and it undulated of its own volition. I looked into the water and admired the most beautiful koi I had ever see—

Ack! I can't breathe! Oh my Goddess Brid, I'm drowning! I am not supposed to be in a lake. Nor in any water. A little waterfall is one thing, but I am not Coralie! I'm a spring fae. I am the queen of the spring fae of Gwynf'l! Ack! I can't breathe!

I gulped for air but all that I ingested was water.

Goddess Brid, I'm drowning! Help!

My vision went black, and my whole body was becoming numb. Then I felt myself being pulled by the collar of the white robe, trying to gasp for air on the side of a foreign lake. I heard yelling in some language I didn't understand. It sounded choppy yet sing-songy.

While I was doing my best to spit water out of my lungs and pull air back into them, I heard Tang yelling at someone in that foreign dialect. He grabbed the woman in the flat black jacket and long braid with one hand by the shoulders and was shaking her and wagging a finger in front of her face.

WU

"Mai Li! Are you crazy! What do you think you were doing?"

My apprentice just pushed Teeny Weeny into Tiger Pond! If Tiger Pond were just any normal pond, and Siobhan—Teeny Weeny—were just any normal person, it would not have been a catastrophe. But this was not the case! Tiger Pond was sacred! Xiānnǚ were sacred! Had I not taught Mai Li anything?

"Mai Li! Do you realize that if she died, the ruler would execute you for killing her? Not to mention execute me, as she is necessary to cure their son? I fear you have lost your mind!"

"I'm sorry, Master Wu!" she kowtowed to me. "She is trying to steal you from me!"

"I am not yours to be stolen, Mai Li. You are my apprentice, and you have been a fine one thus far. You should be proud of what you have learned and how you can help our people. But this is unforgivable!"

TEENY WEENY

The woman in black crumpled to the ground, crying and pulling at the hem of Tang's robe. It looked as if she was begging for forgiveness, and even though I could not speak their language, I was positive that was the crux of the confrontation.

"Stop, Tang!" I hollered at the top of my water-soaked lungs. *Father, Gruff-Grenfold, Mother Rose, Coralie—everything! Amends, forgiveness. That is what the centuries need to survive. I see it now!* "We have a mission! We need to do it now!"

~

WU

I grabbed Mai Li by the arm and led her to the palace. Siobhan, bless the little fae, seemed to have recovered from the Mai Li incident and was right behind us. Even more astounding, she was still holding her perfectly wonderful wand, clutched in both hands. *That's a woman who knows how to focus on a mission.*

~

TEENY WEENY

I was standing in the massive bedroom, the one that was described as the prince's chambers. There was a reflecting shield, not exactly a mirror, more a finely polished sheet of silver, and I saw myself now as the others saw me. The white robe I found myself cloaked in was embellished with multicolored starbursts, just like the ones that seemed to flow in and out of every strand of my now totally white hair.

Tang appeared exactly as I saw him in my visions. He was wearing his crane robe, a small cap upon his head of pure white locks. The more recent closely cropped fu manchu of Dr. Timothy Wu was now a long mustache that melded into an even longer snowy goatee.

Mai Li was holding a flask of teal-colored water, and Tang plucked a hair from his own goatee, placing it in the flask. He nodded at me.

It's my turn, again.

I took out my wand, which also seemed to have undergone its own transformation. It fit into my hands perfectly, but the shaft felt like it was made of alabaster, rather than the wood I was used to handling. *I have to let go. If I overthink this, I will get it wrong, that I am sure of.*

I murmured a prayer under my breath:

Please, Goddess Brid, be my hand and sight

And touch this task with your guiding light

The small orb at the tip of my wand began to glow brilliantly. Suddenly, the entire room was filled with a blinding white light. Not even the smallest corner of the room was spared a shadow.

The mixture in the flask became effervescent, popping with tiny champagne-like bubbles. Tang took the flask from Mai Li and gently pressed it to the lips of the pale prince. The liquid trickled into his mouth as we all held our breath, hoping and waiting.

Color slowly began to flow back into the child's skin, a pink blush appearing on his cheeks. His long black eyelashes fluttered, then his eyes opened wide. He took in the sight of his mother and father, peered at Tang and Mai Li, then looked at me. He smiled gently and said something in Chinese.

Tang laughed and turned to me and translated. "He said '*Xiānnǚ?* What are you doing here?' I told you he was gifted."

WU

We left the prince and his parents to celebrate his regained health. Both Siobhan and I were exhausted. Especially my precious fae, for not only did she come from far away into a land completely unknown to her, but she nearly drowned in the process.

I escorted her to the guest quarters of the palace after the emperor gave us leave and commanded we meet him and the empress in the throne room in the morning.

I could not help myself. I opened the door to the guest chamber for her, and I was not sure what came over me, but as I looked into those deep hazel eyes, gold flecks flashing about, I could not help but place my hand under her chin and lift her face up to mine. I gently kissed her soft lips.

She was obviously taken aback, and I was afraid that I had overstepped my bounds. She had taken a small jump backwards. I could not tell if she was astonished, insulted, or what. Then she gave me a quick peck on the cheek and said goodnight, hurriedly shutting the door behind her.

I supposed that was a good sign.

I had been the rulers' shaman for some thirty years now. Never had I cared for anything but my profession and my people, but now it was different. I thought I would like nothing better but to spend as much time with this tiny lady as she would possibly allow. I doubted I could convince her to stay here, so I was at a loss.

~

TEENY WEENY

Oh my goddesses, he kissed me! It was frightening and wonderful all at the same time. What was I to do now? He lived in a time and place that was so foreign to me. If only there were some way he could come back to Havenwood Falls. Of course, he might not want to come back. After all, this was his life here, and Havenwood Falls must have been so foreign to him. Although, he did fit in pretty well as Dr. Timothy Wu.

Well, I was just dreaming. We each had our own place and time to be, and they were not together, at least not anymore.

~

WU

We were all gathered in the throne room. Even the young prince sat beside his father on a smaller throne.

My teeny weeny fae looked as if she had had little sleep last night. I myself did not sleep well. I tossed and turned, dismayed that today would be our last day together.

The emperor raised his hand. Everyone became still and silent before he spoke.

"Tang Da Wu, you have served the kingdom well as our Royal Wu. You have not only saved our child, but the future of the dynasty. For this you deserve a reward. What is your wish?"

Well, I certainly wasn't expecting that. I had done many things for the rulers and for the people over the decades, but never had I been rewarded. It was my job; the satisfaction in that was reward enough.

If only the emperor could wave his staff or his mighty sword and make it so Siobhan and I could be together.

"Your highnesses! I thank you for your generosity. It has been many years that I have been nothing other than your wizard. That has been all I had ever wanted, and it has been my pleasure always to serve you and the kingdom. However, if I were to wish for anything, I wish that I could spend all the rest of my days with this little *Xiānnǚ*, if she would allow me."

The young prince smiled and nodded his agreement. The empress stood behind him, patting him on the shoulders in affirmation.

"Who would take your place?" the emperor asked, contemplating the request, but I felt unsure that he was liable to grant it.

"Mai Li can take my place as the Royal Wu, your excellency. She has been under my tutelage for well over fifteen years, and is ready to become a Master Wu."

The empress was delighted with this suggestion. I believe she was keen on the idea of the palace wizard being a woman for a change.

"Father," the young prince spoke up, "Tang Da Wu is the best Wu ever, but I think he will be an unhappy Wu if he is not with the one he loves. Mai Li is fair and kind to me, and I've seen her in practice. She can do this. Please, Father!"

The love and compassion that was bestowed upon the boy by the great spirits shone even more brightly at that moment. He said "the one he loves," and I knew he was completely right. *I do love Siobhan.*

"Very well. Make your preparations. Your wish is granted if the *Xiānnǚ* will have you."

We bowed to the rulers, all three of them, and were dismissed with a wave of the emperor's hand.

～

TEENY WEENY

"What was all that about? I heard you say *Xiānnǚ* several times. You were talking about me?"

"The emperor asked me what I wish as a reward for curing his son. I told them I wished for nothing more than to spend the rest of my days with you, if you would have me."

"Well, I don't know if I would have you or not. But I do know I have to go back to Havenwood Falls. That is my home, my family, and I must go back soon."

He looked at me in such a heartbroken manner, I was choking up, but I blurted out anyway, "Would you come to Havenwood Falls with me?"

"Why yes, of course! But I would not know how. It is one thing to occupy another person's body for a short period of time, but I certainly could not do it for the rest of my life. That would be unconscionable."

I looked down at the ground and made little circles in the dirt path with my foot as we stood outside the palace. I did not want Tang to see the tears welling up in my eyes.

"Let us go sit by Tiger Pond. There is great power that emits from the temple, and the Great Spirit Crane may descend upon us to give us some guidance. At the very least, we will have these moments together."

His words were soft and gentle, but I could hear and feel the pain, so much like mine. He took my hand in his and led me to the temple in the forest. We sat at the edge of the pond on a finely hewn stone bench. I stared into the dark blue-violet waters of the pond, watching the koi swim lazily around on a course only they understood.

I closed my eyes, trying to hold back the tears, so much like the ache I felt when I rippled to Gwynf'l only to find that I could not change that history and learning there was more to my mother's death and my father's pain.

When I opened my eyes, the tears that had welled up blurred the purplish pool before me, and I saw it! The answer!

"Tang, I think I can take you back with me!"

"In your ripple?"

"No, in a portal! My portal! It might work! I hope it will work!"

"Great Spirit Crane has blessed you with inspiration! Thank you, Great Spirit!"

"And thank my Goddess Brid!"

I told him about the wand and how I accidentally formed a portal that led me from Gwynf'l back to my own bedroom, and how it seemed to have an effect on my hair, I guess to warn him. Then I just burst out laughing at myself for even mentioning it. This was not the Timothy Wu who appeared in Havenwood Falls. I was looking at Tang, my Tang, whose hair was already totally white.

I touched my wand to my nose, concentrating on the memory of my bedroom with the purple portal next to the wardrobe. The blast resounded throughout the forest, and the bolts appeared as if a giant amethyst had just exploded. An undulating circular opening appeared before us, the same dark violet that I knew waited on the other side.

"Take my hand!" I said to him, and without hesitation, he did.

We walked into the portal together, Tang gripping my left hand tightly as I hung on to my wand with my right. We entered the swirling mist of colorful sparks that wound us through the dark purple vortex, whooshing us to our destination.

EPILOGUE

TEENY WEENY

*E*veryone was gathered in the parlor, while Cyllene and I were in the kitchen. I was preparing some teacakes and little sandwiches for everyone to snack on. I could hear the pixie sisters yammering to Mat and Nina about how Wu and I were both going to teach at the "Sun & Moon Academy of Guardian something or other," as Aeiri was calling it.

Cyllene was staring at the rainbow that was weaving in and out of my snow-white head of hair.

"I know, Silly Annie, I'm going to have to glamour it back to my normal brown. I can't very well go around town with all this racket going on in my hair. Funny how Tang's hair came out a purplish black color. He almost looks like when he arrived as Timothy Wu, save for needing a bit of trim on that beard and mustache."

Cyllene nodded in agreement, flying behind me as I carried the tray of treats into the parlor. Wu was on the settee before the hearth, and Mat stood behind Nina, who had her legs curled up in the overstuffed chair.

"I'm sorry about you girls not getting admitted to the Academy," I said, not really sorry at all. "I'm sure there is something we can find for you to help out with, though."

"It's okay," replied Enya.

"Yeah, we decided to start our own Pixie University," stated Tierri.

"We're going to call it P.U. for short," spoke up Ushka.

Then Aeiri began to giggle and blurted out, "Yeah, like P.U., you stink!"

That started the ruckus, the pixies all saying "you stink" to one another, a rabbit punch here and there, and the next moment they were rolling all over the floor wrestling one another.

Mat cautiously stepped over a couple of wrestling pixies and knelt on one knee before Nina. He took her hand in his, looked into those big black eyes of hers, and said, "Nina, would you please be my wife, and share this humble owl's life?"

My breath caught. Cyllene stopped in midair and nearly fell to the ground, and even the pixie sisters came to an abrupt halt. All of us waited anxiously for Nina to answer.

"Si! Si! Mio bel gufo! My handsome owl! I thought you would never ask!"

The pixies became a band of cheerleaders, whooping and hollering, doing somersaults and all kinds of acrobatics, making up songs about weddings and flowers and bells and bows.

Mat beamed with joy, and I looked at Tang, who had a big smile on his face.

Did I just see a twinkle in Tang's eyes? Uh oh, there goes that tingling feeling in my fingers, lobes, nose, and toes again!

~

We hope you enjoyed this story in the Havenwood Falls series featuring a variety of supernatural creatures. The series is a collaborative effort by multiple authors. You might also enjoy T.V. Hahn's other stories in the Havenwood Falls universe:
The Winged & the Wicked
The Ward & the Wanderers

You may also enjoy these books in the main Havenwood Falls series:

Flames Among the Frost by Amy Hale
Rock Me Gently by Susan Burdorf
From the Embers by Amy Miles
Defying Gravity by Kallie Ross
How the Dead Lie by Stacey Rourke

Also look for the YA line, Havenwood Falls High; the historical paranormal line, Legends of Havenwood Falls; the sexier side of town, Havenwood Falls Sin & Silk; the local supernatural college, Sun & Moon Academy; and the Havenwood Falls holiday short story anthologies.

Stay up to date at www.HavenwoodFalls.com

ABOUT THE AUTHOR

T.V. Hahn has loved the fantastical and whimsical since she was a child, which may or may not have been that long ago. A creative soul, she enjoys making art with her hands, her voice, and her words. She finds humor in everything and is the first to laugh at her own jokes. During her downtime, you may find her tending her floral beauties, writing poetry, working on her faerie gardens, or watching *The Dark Crystal* or *The Princess Bride*. All of this, combined with her petite stature, has made more than one person wonder if she is, indeed, a faerie. It may be no accident that her first published book is about Teeny Weeny Tahini, a spring fae living in Havenwood Falls. Hahn is self-employed and lives in Florida with her husband and pup. She can be reached through her publisher, Ang'dora Productions.

ACKNOWLEDGMENTS

My readers, who I know are loyal and put up with me being "invisible," thank you for your reviews and your enthusiasm, and I hope I can cast some faerie dust your way.

Regina, for getting Dr. Timothy Wu spot on for the cover!

All the great writers in Havenwood Falls who share so much, and the SUPER characters that make it so exciting and fun.

Our publisher who works tirelessly to make Havenwood Falls the place all of us want to be!

To Paul, who supports me, gives me the time off needed (and some I don't really need but want), and helps me put it all together (even reading about faeries).

AN EXCERPT

~ A Havenwood Falls New Adult Novella ~

HAVENWOOD FALLS

A DEMON'S REDEMPTION

JD NELSON

A Demon's Redemption (A Havenwood Falls Novella) by J.D. Nelson

How far are you willing to go to win back the person you love? For someone as desperate as Rayonus, the answer is pretty damn far.

For six hundred years, demon Rayonus Rixa has used the threat of his destructive power to fund his nomadic, mercenary lifestyle and hasn't had the time or inclination to care about someone other than himself. The day the demon hierarchy tasked him with a job unlike any other, that all changed, and in turn, he changed. Whether that was for the better was debatable until the moment he met the person who made him stop in his tracks.

Penelope Osbourne was unlike anyone he had ever met—sassy, beautiful, and a little crazy for her favorite TV angel. He knew she would be it for him. In Penelope, he finally found a future that didn't include death or general mayhem. Then, in typical demon fashion, he promptly screwed it up ten ways to Sunday.

With nothing left to lose, Rayonus sets out to do the impossible by any means necessary, and if that means he has to become a model citizen of Havenwood Falls, then that's what he'll do. For her, he will do anything.

A DEMON'S REDEMPTION

BY JD NELSON

Every demon has a breaking point, and as it turns out, my breaking point was the sixty-seventh time Penelope Osbourne told me to go fuck myself.

She didn't even ease me into it. She verbally pounced on me while I was waiting to cross the street at Main and Eighth, chewed me up, and spit me out as if I wasn't worth the effort it took to swallow. All I could do was stare as she stormed away, the fury and heat of a thousand suns in her usually cheerful brown eyes.

And, to think, before I came along, she used to be such a nice woman.

"How does one go about redeeming oneself?" I asked aloud, throwing myself onto the nearest bench and burying my head in my hands. I was tired, so tired, of trying and failing. My confidence was shaken to my core. And for me—hell, for any demon—that was really saying something.

To my surprise, someone answered my exhausted query. "In my experience, you start with flowers and work your way up to the hard stuff."

Mouth quirked into a suppressed grin, I looked up to find a violet-eyed woman with a sleek silver-blond bob smiling down at me. I hadn't realized anyone had been close enough to overhear me, but I guess I should've. This was Havenwood Falls, after all. I knew to expect the unexpected when dealing with its citizens.

Sliding over, I offered the lady a seat next to me on the park bench and asked, "Do you have much experience in redeeming yourself?"

She grinned as she sat. "No, but I do have experience with flowers. My sister, Reagan, and I own Fairy Tale Florists over on Fifth Street."

"Well, if you're willing to help me out of a hopeless, no chance of succeeding, ridiculously horrible situation, I'm willing to try anything." I stuck out my hand. "I'm Rayonus Rixa."

"Rhiannon Underwood. Nice to meet you, Rayonus."

"Likewise," I told her, genuinely meaning it. "So, tell me a little more about how this flowers-to-redemption thing works. Because for the life of me, I cannot get the hostile woman I love to see me as more than someone who has betrayed her trust."

"I saw that, and I have to ask—do you deserve to be seen as anything more than that?"

I sighed, staring down at my black leather boots, embarrassed, not for the first time, that I had been such a schmuck. "Truthfully, Rhiannon, in the beginning, I didn't."

She nodded in understanding. "But you're different now?"

"Decidedly so." I met her kind eyes. She was so easy to talk to; I felt compelled to tell her the truth. "I feel absolutely nothing but remorse for what I've done. I love her. I'll never do anything to hurt Penelope again."

And it was true. Every single word of it.

Seemingly satisfied with the honesty in my answer, Rhiannon said, "Well, Rayonus, I think I can help you. Or, at least, I can try."

Sighing in relief, I gave her a grateful smile. "You're too kind."

"Nonsense," she said, waving away my gratitude. "You can thank me when *and if* you get back into your Penelope's good graces."

"I will do that," I told her, suppressing another grin. I was going to like Rhiannon Underwood.

After a few more minutes of chatting, Rhiannon invited me to walk with her from the town square to her flower shop, a dark gray three-story Victorian with whimsical eggplant purple trim, complete with turrets and an odd, beguiling charm that made me feel instantly at home. The interior was just as delightful, with colorful butterflies and small chirping birds flying about the lush greenery and flowers in perfect harmony.

I stood still, nearly gaping at the enchanting sight. "This is lovely."

"Thank you," she said, gesturing to a petite brunette with striking blue-green eyes behind the counter. "Allow me to introduce my sister, Reagan Fairchild. Reagan, this is Rayonus Rixa."

"How do you do, Mr. Rixa?" Reagan asked.

"I am very well, now that your kind sister has agreed to help me in my quest to win back the heart of my beloved."

Brows raised, Reagan gave her sister a quizzical look and stuck a pencil behind her ear. "Has she? Then I wish you luck."

"I need all the luck I can get," I told her, noticing the *Help Wanted* sign displayed next to her. "And speaking of that, are you, by chance, still hiring?"

"Yes, we are. Are you in search of a job?"

I nodded. "Sadly, my job giving the occasional ghost tour doesn't quite allow me to pay my way. I've been living off my savings and staying with friends until something steadier comes along."

"Well, if you can be reliable and show up on time, I think Reagan and I can give you a shot," Rhiannon said. "On a trial basis, of course."

"Of course. Thank you. You don't know how much I appreciate everything you're doing for me."

She winked. "You should. This will give you the perfect opportunity to see your Penelope."

Grinning conspiratorially, I said, "I see you and I are of the same mind."

Interest piqued, Reagan fingered the fine pearls around her neck and asked, "Is Penelope your beloved?"

"Yes. It may be an impossible task, but I'm trying to earn back her trust, and hopefully, her regard."

Reagan nodded sagely. "Then you're going to need roses. Rhiannon's arrangements have a way of changing even the hardest of hearts."

I retrieved my wallet from my back pocket and pulled out my debit card. "You'd better ring me up for a few dozen, because, after what I've done, this particular heart may be a little harder than most."

~

I left Fairy Tale Florists and headed home feeling both lighter and conflicted. While delivering flowers for the ladies would give me a much-needed chance to see Penelope outside of her job at the Chinese buffet, it was also just a front—one that made me feel like a great big douche for lying about my circumstances to the ladies to get the job. It was true I did need steady employment, but it was only for appearance's sake. I didn't need money. After six hundred years of devious deals and double-crossing demon activity, I'd amassed quite a bit of wealth and wouldn't be strapped for cash for the next millennium or so. What I was strapped for was a reason to stay in town. The more Penelope saw me around, making an effort to call Havenwood Falls my home and not just my occasional crash pad, the better.

I shook my head as I internally berated myself. It seemed funny to me now—the way I used to be. I had been the most cunning and deceptive demon I knew, save for a few megalomaniacal examples. There hadn't been a creature—demon, human, or otherwise—that I cared one fig about. Then I met Penelope, and everything started to change. I started to change. My priorities, once selfish and self-centered, were becoming focused on the one thing that really mattered —the sweet and funny half-demon woman that had no inkling she wasn't one hundred percent human.

Sadly, as much as I had wanted to do the right thing by her, my careless, reckless demon nature made a wreck of everything. Once I had gained everything I wanted in Penelope—her reluctant admiration, her trust—I traded it all away on a crazy roundabout plan that nearly got her killed because I was prone to go into every situation with guns blazing instead of thinking about what the outcome could end up being.

Kidnapping her? Taking her to be imprisoned (however temporarily) by a demon I knew wouldn't care if she ended up a casualty? I honestly didn't know what I had been thinking, and if she never forgave me, I wouldn't blame her.

Purchase *A Demon's Redemption* where books are sold.

www.ingramcontent.com/pod-product-compliance
Lightning Source LLC
Chambersburg PA
CBHW052006170626
46808CB00007B/2793